Frisked by You

SAPD SWAT

Book 6

Nikki Mays

Nikki Mays

Published by Nikki Mays

Cover Design: Crystal Green @ Kingston Publishing Designs

Photographer: Reggie Deanching @ RplusMphoto

Cover Model: Scott Holliday @ The Stable & Models of RplusMphoto

Editing: Golden Life Publishing

Formatting: T.L. Mason

Dedication

I want to thank everyone who has supported me throughout this series. The list is too long to write. First and foremost, my husband Billy. You're unwavering support and faith in me helps keep me going when I feel like I'm failing. You pick me up and give me the confidence to keep writing. You may be my annoyance, but you're truly my forever!

Thank you to my family, especially my parents for your continued encouragement. I love that you make sure to buy all my books...even if you don't seem to get around to reading them. Hint hint mother.

To all of my readers...you guys kick ass...period! You all make this dream a reality for me.

To my wonderful and brillant editor Brooke, girl I would be so lost without you. You came into my life at book three and I don't know how I survived the first two without you. You are truly amazing and always know how to polish my words to make them pretty and not the ramblings of an over caffeinated momma.

To Reggie...Panda, thank you so much for your support and wisdom that you are always willing to share with me. You never expect anything in return, well maybe for me to buy a new picture...J/K. But I can not express how much I value having you in my life, even if my bank account hates you, I adore you and your amazing pictures.

Table of Contents

Are fat rolls really so bad? I mean everyone has them when they sit down...right? Okay, granted I have them when I'm standing too, but still. Is it really worth being thin if I have to eat salad and grilled chicken all the damn time?

I look down at my very unappetizing salad and sigh. Pushing it away, I stare at Stacy's steaming pizza. Lucky bitch is a size two and eats everything in sight. If she wasn't the nicest person that I've ever met I would totally hate her.

The worst part is, that even with dieting and exercise, I've only managed to lose three pounds in the last two months. Yup, that's right, three measly fucking pounds after depriving myself of anything that tastes like it was meant to be in my mouth.

The thought sounded dirty in my mind and I can't help the chuckle that slips out of my mouth. Dirty thoughts are the most excitement my love life has seen in the past year, okay well over a year and a half. Alright, it may be closer to two years but who's counting? Certainly not me and my empty, lonesome bed...that's for sure.

Ah, the little lies that make me feel less pathetic. If this keeps up, I'm going to end up with a shit load of cats, which would suck since I'm allergic to nasty little furballs. Seriously, I have never met a cat that I like and the feeling is totally mutual, they hate me just as much.

"Can you stop staring at me like that?" Stacy asks with a frown on her overly perfect face.

Have I mentioned that my work bestie is the epitome of perfection? Natural blonde hair, pale blue eyes, huge pink lips, button nose and a body that I would literally sell my soul for. And on top of all of that, she is the sweetest and most down to earth human on the planet.

"Like what?" I question. Not realizing that I was actively staring at her.

"You keep looking at me and licking your lips."

I grimace. "I'm not looking at you, I'm looking at your pizza."

She snorts. "I know, but it's creepy all the same."

"Sorry," I mumble and look around the cafeteria while she finishes her food.

Luckily the hospital cafeteria is full of people to watch. There is never a dull moment, whether it's doctors clinging together or nurses and everyone else talking shit about the ones that they can't stand.

Stacy and I are nurses in the E.D. or Emergency Department. We both make sure to leave the floor for lunch or we would never actually get to take a break. There is always someone who needs "just one thing" and then before you know it, your shift is over without a break. I've learned the hard way to run as fast as I can when I'm given a break.

I start to watch a couple who are having an obvious dispute. The woman is a radiology tech and the guy is in transport according to their badges. The longer that I watch, the more animated the woman becomes. Oh, she is angry and is waving her hands around wildly, causing me to giggle.

"What's so funny?" Stace asks.

I tilt my head in the direction of the couple. "This chick looks like she's about to go nuclear on this idiot."

Stacey looks and starts shaking her head. "That's her own fault. Everyone knows not to seriously date any of the guys in transport. They all get around, literally and figuratively."

I nod my head and keep watching the couple, even though he's now walking away. She's following right after him like a dog with a bone. Stacey is right though. Everyone knows that the guys in transport tend to "talk" to like four or five different women at once.

They always make sure that the women are on different floors, but it still eventually gets found out. My guess is, that's what's going on here. This chick just found out that she's not the only one.

My phone starts vibrating in my scrub top pocket interrupting my thoughts. I take it out and see that it's time for us to get back to the floor already. I sigh loudly and Stace looks at me.

"Is it time already?" she grumbles.

"Yep," I reply blandly.

We both get up and clean up all of the trash from the table that we were sitting at. We throw everything into the garbage and proceed to leave the cafeteria.

The hospital itself is actually extremely large and takes up about two city blocks. So, at least it will take us a few minutes to get back to the E.D. Some days you really just have to mentally prepare yourself.

Don't get me wrong, I love my job. There is nothing else that I would rather do. But the patients and some of my coworkers can make it really trying some days. And it never fails that I get at least one crazy patient, a drug seeker or just a general pervert at least once a week, if not more. It really takes a lot to keep my mouth shut and not slap people. I'm not overly violent, but some people make me imagine that I am.

Luckily, it's almost four o'clock at night, which means I only have another three hours until the end of my shift. I snort. Well, four, maybe four and a half by the time I give my relief report. Oh, the joys of having to switch off and give someone else a report. It's generally a miracle if they're on time too.

I can't understand why my relief is always late. It's night time for fuck's sakes! It's not like they are trying to get here in rush hour traffic! There is nothing that I hate more than being ready to get the hell out of here after a long shift, only to have to wait for the moron replacing me. My teeth unintentionally grind just thinking about it.

Heather is the worst too. I know that she does it on purpose. She and I aren't exactly close. Okay, we hate each other's guts. If she was on fire and I had a bottle of water, I would drink it in front of her and keep on walking. I know, I know, I sound horrible. But that bitch is the reason that I've been single for a while.

It's hard to get over the fact that my now ex-fiancée and ex-best friend/maid of honor were having sex for months right under my nose. I try to be a good person but Mother Theresa I am not. Finding them in my bed, in my apartment, was just the icing on the shit cake they made me.

Thank God I found out before I had put down any non-refundable deposits for the wedding. To think that a few days later I would've been screwed out of my man and my cash. Admittedly, I think I would've gone batshit about the money.

All I did when I found them was kick them out of my place. I then also tossed out all of Aaron's belongings, possibly onto the street, and watched them scramble to pick everything up. I made a recording of that one for everyone to enjoy.

I played it once they announced to the whole hospital two days later that they were getting married. No one cared about them, but I still get high-fives for the video. Did I mention that Aaron is one of the surgeons here? Yep, it's so wonderful to see these two all the damn time. I'm so proud of myself for not going all stabby some days.

We walk through the doors of the E.D. and can hear a loud commotion. In one of the stalls, there are several large police officers in all of their gear. I

10

can hear the man, who I'm guessing is the patient slurring out that he's fine and wants to just go home. And I just know, know it down to my very marrow, that I'm going to get stuck with this guy.

I have no doubt that the last few hours of my shift will be me taking care of this guy who is probably high as a freaking kite. I mean why else would so many police officers be standing around him? I think to myself. This guy must be trouble if he needs so many huge ass guards.

Not that I mind, the cops are beyond gorgeous. It will definitely not be a hardship looking at these guys for the next few hours. Although, looking at all of their fingers, they all seem to be married. Pity, the hot ones are always taken. Oh well, I can still look at all the nice man candy standing in front of me.

I nudge Stacey with my arm. "How much you want to bet that I end up with this guy as my patient?" I mumble trying not to move my lips too much.

"Honey, if you don't want to take this patient, I'll switch with you. I have absolutely no problem being stuck near all that raw maleness," she says while fanning herself.

I roll my eyes and push her away from me as I make my way back to the nurses' station. I look at the charts and it was just as I suspected, the guy in four is all mine. How do I get so lucky?

I look over his intake and see that he's a stabbing victim. He's already been given some pretty strong pain meds, which would explain his slurred speech.

I grab a few supplies and make my way over to him. As I approach, several pairs of male eyes turn towards me. I'm usually not the shrinking violet type, but I can't help but feel unnerved by all the attention. Especially the one who is ginormous and gives me a creepy blank stare. Geez, aren't cops supposed to be a little friendly?

They all automatically part as I get near and I can't help but think how weird it is. It's like they all share a damn brain or something. Walking over, I slide the curtain back and my hand freezes as I take in the patient in the bed.

The gorgeous man is identical to the creepy guy behind me. The wheels in my head begin to spin as I take in his appearance.

Shirtless, his golden sun-kissed skin screams of a natural tan. My eyes quickly dart over his muscular arms and rock hard abs. I swallow hard when his piercing eyes connect with my own. The goofy smile on his face is no doubt courtesy of the pain meds. Even in his current state, he's the most magnificent man that I have ever seen.

Noticing that he's also wearing the same type of pants that the other police officers are, I conclude that he's a cop and not a criminal as I had originally thought. For some reason it makes me feel a lot better. Not that I'm biased but it sucks having to be so on guard when we get people in here under police custody. You just never know what to expect with them.

"Hi, you must be Declan. My name is Aimee and I'll be your nurse for the next few hours."

He's holding a blood-soaked bandage to his side but still looks completely relaxed lying here. His eyes snap to mine when I speak and his grin gets even wider. I have a feeling that he means it to be a sexy smirk but in his current state, he's not pulling it off very well.

"Well, helloooo," he slurs horribly and wobbles to his side.

The giggle I try to hold back slips from behind my lips. The man who I assume is his twin walks past me and rights his brother. "Lie back you idiot before you hurt yourself," he grunts out.

"Move!" Declan tries but fails to swat his brother out of his way. "I want to see the hot nurse."

Ignoring his comment, I glance over the chart and take my readings.

"Do you think that she'll give me a sponge bath? Maybe she'll let me give her a sponge bath. We can both soap each other up and have some fun."

I can feel my face turn red at his suggestion. Trying to remain as professional as possible, I busy myself with my tasks. But I can't pretend like the words didn't have an effect on me. My self-confidence took a little hit when I found out that I was getting cheated on. Hearing his words boosted my confidence a smidge.

I can hear the other guys making coughing sounds that suspiciously sound like laughs but I just ignore it. Declan probably can't help what he's saying at this point with the number of drugs that he was given for pain. I look up at his brother, who is somehow managing to keep a straight face. Though, I swear, I can see the corner of his lips twitching.

The creepy twin tilts his head in his brother's direction. "Sorry about him. You don't have to worry though, he's extremely dumb and harmless."

I just shrug as I put a pair of gloves on. "It's okay. Not the worst thing that has ever been said about me. Plus, he can't help it right now. When the drugs wear off, he'll be back to normal."

I walk over to my way too handsome patient. Seriously, who looks this good after getting stabbed? Lifting the bandage to inspect his wounds, I pause when he grabs my forearm. I gasp as his touch sends a jolt of electricity through me.

Jesus, I really need to get laid if a simple touch is causing me to think shit like this. So what if he's the hottest man that I have ever seen in my life and has abs that look photoshopped. There is absolutely no reason for me to be having these thoughts. Now if my panties would stop becoming damper by the second, that would be awesome.

Declan leans his face into mine. The move should frighten me, he's huge after all and has me in a tight grip, but it doesn't. Lord help me, getting away from him is the last thing on my mind. I can also see his brother take a step closer out of the corner of my eye.

Declan has the goofy grin on his face, with excited eyes. Good grief, women probably just drop their panties and beg for his attention. "Are you going to frisk me?"

It takes me a few moments to process what he just asked and all I can do is blink. "What?" I sputter out.

He looks at me so earnestly that I know he's going to kick himself for this one when the drugs wear off. "Are you going to frisk me? Because if you are, it's only fair that I get to do the same," he says while wiggling his eyebrows.

I can't help the laugh that tumbles out of my mouth. "Do you want me to frisk you?"

He nods his head eagerly like a little boy agreeing to more chocolate. "Yes please."

"Jesus, Dec," his twin mutters and looks at me again. "I swear he's harmless. I think that mom just dropped him on his head a few times when we were kids."

I give his twin a smile and pat Declan's face. "It's okay, I'm sure he's not like this when he's not drugged up."

I receive a few snorts to that. Another gorgeous one who looks like a giant steps forward. "Oh no, he's always this dumb, but at least now we get to document it properly." It takes me a minute to realize that he has his phone pointed at Declan.

I cluck my tongue at him. "That's so mean. He can't even help it right now."

They all turn to me without an ounce of remorse anywhere on their faces. The oldest one steps forward. "He could help it if he wasn't stubborn and hadn't decided to go off half-cocked." The words sound like a growl coming from his throat.

I would definitely not want to be on the receiving end of that tone. Declan just snorts without care. "I told you already. You all have wives and kids and need to make it home safe. I don't have anyone."

He shrugs casually. "No one cares if I make it home or not. It's better to have something happen to me instead of one of you guys." He lays his head back and promptly falls asleep. And it's surprising to me that he lasted as long as he did.

His words are the saddest that I've ever heard and I can begin to feel my broken and beat up heart fall a little in love with him.

I knew I should've faked a stomach bug and skipped the rest of my shift.

Slowly I awake to a sharp pain in my side as I take in my unfamiliar surroundings. The beeping machines and monitors let me know that I've somehow landed in the hospital. My mind races with questions.

What the hell happened last night? How drunk did I get?

Trying to lift my head to get a better idea of where I am, I'm suddenly hit with another sharp pain. Why does everything fucking hurt? Did I get hit by a car or something?

Lying perfectly still, I breathe deeply through my nose. It doesn't stop the pain but the memories come rushing back to me. Shit! I got stabbed by that fucking tweaker holding his kid for ransom money so that he could buy more dope.

Each day I lose a little bit more faith in humanity as a whole. This jackass held his own kid hostage with a huge ass bowie hunting knife...at the bank.

The moron was convinced that they would just hand him over all their money so that he could buy more shit to get high with.

The team and I were there for three hours before we started to move in. The piece of shit had his back to the wall and his little girl in front of him. There was no way to get a clean shot.

Unfortunately, he was starting to come down and was getting desperate for his next fix. His hands were shaking so badly that the knife actually cut into his daughter, Jaylen, in a few places.

Truthfully, I went against protocol and just went in. All I could think was that he was one violent shake away from slitting this little girl's throat. My actions were purely instinctual after that.

I was able to rush him quickly enough to catch him off guard. Luckily, Dam usually knows what I'm about to do before I do it. He was just waiting for his chance to grab the girl and get her out of harm's way.

It worked out well except for me getting stabbed when the jackass went ape shit and just started thrashing around. But all in all, it worked out okay. Better for me to get stabbed than a sweet little girl.

I try to move a bit and groan in pain.

Yeah, moving isn't going to be happening too much. Jesus, my body feels like it's been hit by a Mack truck.

"You awake?" My brother grunts moving the curtain aside. He really needs to find other levels of speaking.

"Yeah," I moan.

My oh-so-loving brother makes a non-committal sound. I know that sound. That sound means he knows something that he can hold over my head. It's enough to make me crack open one eye and then promptly shut it.

"Lights," I gasp.

I hear Dam move and can see the lights dim from underneath my eyelids. "Okay, you can open them now," he states.

I slowly peak one open like the little bitch I am. I open both when I find that he wasn't lying. I wouldn't put it past him to be waiting by the switch just to turn them back on when I open my eyes fully. But luckily for me, he's taken a seat.

"How long have I been out?" I grit my teeth when I try to sit up. I feel like I'm being stabbed all over again, but I say nothing, no need to give my brother any ammunition.

He leans back, as far as his large body can in a tiny, plastic chair that looks like it's about to break under his size and puts his arms behind his head. Making his muscles bulge so much that I'm concerned for his shirt. Someone obviously hasn't been skipping arm day.

"Long enough for them to sew you up and clean the wound. The doctor just wants to talk to you when you're awake and then we can get out of here."

I nod and see the clean bandage on my left side. I look around the small cubicle that we're in and frown. "Where are the rest of the guys?"

Dam's lips twitch. "They left after you passed out after making a fool of yourself in front of your nurse."

I frown at his words. "What are you talking about?" Even as I ask him, a pair of grey eyes surrounded by long, dark chestnut hair is coming back to me.

If my memory is correct, my nurse is a fucking knockout. Long hair, gorgeous eyes, full lips that aren't too big, soft features, large breasts that are definitely a handful and curves that go on for days. Basically, my idea of perfection.

"Is it coming back to you yet?" Dam asks in a mocking tone. Shell and I are the only ones who ever get this side of him. I know why he likes keeping certain parts of himself hidden but he really needs to open up more.

I run my hands up and down my face. I keep my hands covering my eyes but open them a bit to peek out at my brother. "Did I actually ask her to frisk me?" I whine like a toddler who is never going to get the hot nurse of his every future fantasy.

My brother smiles widely. "You also asked her to give you a sponge bath." I groan loudly. "But don't worry, you were feeling very generous and offered to return the favor."

18

"Fuuuck," is all that comes out of my mouth.

"Pretty much," he agrees.

I lower my hands and look at him with hopeful eyes. "Did the guys leave before that?" I ask praying like hell that I might at least have something on my side.

From the look that's telling me that I'm a moron, I'm going to guess not. "Do you really think that they would leave while you were drugged up and slurring out stupid shit?"

"A man can hope," I reply sullenly. I lean my head back on the pillow. "Marc recorded it, didn't he?" I don't even know why I'm bothering to ask. I know damn well that his ass wouldn't pass up a golden opportunity like that.

"Why are you asking stupid questions?"

"Right," I reply. I look at my brother again. "How pissed at me was the hot nurse....?"

My brother easily reads my mind before answering. "Aimee. And she wasn't at all. She laughed it off easily. She even yelled at Marc for recording you and told us that we're all mean."

Sighing, I shake my head. "I'm going to have to apologize." I consider getting her number and asking her on a date to make up for it.

"Good luck."

I narrow my eyes. "Why do you say that?" It's not like I'm a horrible person. If she doesn't want to take me up on a date fine, but she could at least hear me out.

He rolls his eyes like he's listening to my inner monologue, which he very well might be. "She left for the night already."

My eyes widen. "What time is it?"

Dam looks down at his phone. "Half-past eight."

"I've been out that long?"

Dam nods. "Yeah, I guess you needed your beauty sleep."

I ignore the dig. "Maybe my new nurse will be able to tell me her number or something," I muse out loud.

"I doubt it," my handsome twin drawls.

I shake my head. "Don't be such a *Debbie Downer*, I know that it's probably against the rules or some shit. But I can at least give it a try."

Dam sighs. "Not because of that," he grunts. "Because they didn't look too friendly when I saw them near each other. Actually, I was surprised that they didn't kill each other. There is definitely no love lost between them."

"You sure?" I ask out of habit and receive a blank look.

Damon is nothing if not observant. He doesn't speak often but he picks up on everything. He is very much in tune with a person's body language and can usually tell when something is going to go south before it does. It's my guess that they probably hate each other.

It would've been nice to just be able to ask this chick. Damn, now what the hell am I supposed to do? I scratch my head and then immediately lower my arm when I feel the sharp pain. I'm going to have to be more careful about that for a while.

"Just look her up in the system," he tells me.

I give him a look. "You know, I'm beginning to see why everyone says that we're creepy. It can get eerie when you answer all my questions without me having to ask."

He shrugs his massive shoulders carelessly. "Not my problem. Everyone else needs to stop being such whiny bitches."

"Seriously, how in the hell did you land someone like Michelle? It's mind-boggling that she stays with your ass. She could do so much better.

Maybe even be with someone who doesn't act like he has a cactus shoved up his ass most days."

"My dick game is strong," he says so evenly, almost in a bored tone that it takes me a second.

I chuckle and then put my hand over the bandage. "That one was worth the laugh."

"Don't hurt yourself. I don't feel like listening to mom if you reinjure yourself while I'm here."

"Don't act like you don't feel like listening to her complain when we both know that you're scared of her."

He raises an eyebrow. "Says the kiss ass."

I raise my nose and sniff. "It's not my fault that I like treating our mother like gold."

"Uh-huh."

"Where is this new nurse? I'm ready to get the hell out of here," I grumble. For real though, I've been up for at least a half an hour and there has been no sign of this chick.

"Probably still standing at the nurses' station, flirting with some doctor like she was before," Dam drawls.

I give him a sardonic look. "I got a real winner, huh?"

"You did, but she left and stuck you with the whore of the floor."

I smile at him. "You make me so happy to be your twin some days."

He gives me a drool look in return while crossing one leg over his knee. "My life's goal. Whatever will I do now?"

"See, this is why other siblings are better than us. They love each other."

"I haven't killed you after all these years. If that doesn't prove that I love you, I don't know what does," my sentimental other half remarks...yeah other half...it's a twin thing.

"You whisper such sweet things to me. Tell me more, so that I can fall all over myself with gratitude."

He gives me his victorious smirk that screams "*checkmate*" and leans forward. He places his elbows on his knees and stares directly into my eyes. "I memorized her last name for you."

I blink and then blink some more. "I take back every bad thing that I ever said and thought about you. You are by far the world's best brother."

"Yeah," he leans back into the chair again with a smug ass look on his face. "That's what I thought."

Leave it to my brother to not only realize that she's my waking dream. But only he would purposely look at her name tag so that he could memorize her name. All so that I'll be able to find her later on.

Okay, I understand how that last part sounds but it's really not that bad. I'm just going to look her up in the system and possibly give her a call. I'll apologize for being a moron, we'll laugh, I'll ask her out, we'll have great sex, we'll get married, have a ton of kids and live happily ever after. Simple.

I cringe. It sounds absolutely terrible. But in my defense, the memory of her ass in those scrub pants was a thing of true beauty. The song *"Baby Got Back,"* barely compares to what she's got going on. What can I say, I've always been an ass man. And she has the world's juiciest, roundest, most perfect ass that I have ever laid eyes on.

So yes, I will become my brother and most likely stalk this poor woman until she is madly in love with me. I mean, it worked out well for Dam and Shell, so it's bound to work out just as well for me too...easy as pie.

Okay, I have a newfound respect for how much patience my brother has. Well, that and how determined he was that Michelle was the one. Because honestly? This watching and waiting shit is for the damn birds.

Now don't get me wrong, it's not like I'm creeping into her house at night or anything, though I may know where she lives. I'm just casually observing her and waiting for the best time to *"accidentally"* bump into her. There's no real harm in that.

The only infuriating part of this is watching so many assholes practically break their damn necks trying to get a glimpse of her ass. I don't know how Damon managed not to kill any of the dipshits that came onto Michelle. I swear he has the patience of a saint. I will never make fun of him for his commitment ever again.

Admitting to myself, that's probably a lie, but it will be a hell of a long time until I do. I don't understand how he never went on a damn rampage. And her ex getting hit by that car doesn't count. That was just karma doing her thing finally.

So, here I sit in my truck, like the creepy bastard that I've become, watching her run errands on her day off. Surprisingly, it was Marc who actually got me all of her information. I think it was a thank you for making sure that his family didn't shank his whiny ass during his recovery.

What I've learned is that Aimee Kaslowski is an only child. She is twenty-seven years old. Has a Bachelors in nursing and graduated with full honors. She has a male roommate named Brad, who I found out after some digging is very gay. She was engaged two years ago to a doctor at the hospital that she works at and has been single since. She has never been married and doesn't have any children.

I think that at this point, I would actually put Damon to shame. The more I know about her, the more I like her too. She has one other friend that she hangs out with named Stacey who is her opposite in looks. The two of them actually remind me of Mel and Shell when they're together.

"Are you ever going to do this? Or are we just going to waste years of our lives like Damon did?" Marc asks from my side.

I look over and see him gnawing on a Slim Jim. I scrunch my nose up at the disgusting sight. "I'm just waiting for the right time," I explain for the millionth time.

He rolls his eyes and lowers his baseball cap. "Well, you might want to do something soon because that muscle head who would make Mason look small seems to be hitting on her pretty well."

I do a double-take and sure enough, there is some meathead hitting on my future wife. "Jesus, what the fuck? How many steroids can one person take? All he needs is some green paint and his ass could be the *Hulk.*

Everyone's favorite accomplice chuckles from my right. "You better hurry up then, otherwise, before you know, he'll be sharing his protein shakes and much more with her."

"Asshole," I mutter under my breath as I hop out of the truck.

"I heard that!" I hear as I close the door. He really does have some freakish hearing.

I casually stroll, okay maybe I hurry, across the street and *"accidentally"* on purpose knock into *"roid rage"* in my hustle to get across. What? I didn't want to be hit by any of the cars that don't seem to be passing right now.

"My bad," I say and look up *"completely"* shocked to see Aimee standing there.

"Watch it," the behemoth growls.

I can see the exact moment that Aimee realizes who I am. I can also see a few gears turning in her head too. I should probably be afraid. When a woman's mind is moving that quickly, it's not usually a good thing for any guy that's around.

"Hey babe, I'm glad that you finally made it," Aimee says while imploring me with her eyes to go along with her.

It's like fate is on my side. I don't even need to try for an opening...she's actually giving it to me. And people say that stalking doesn't pay off. I give her an apologetic grin and put my arms around her. "I'm sorry sweetheart, Marc decided that he needed help with something. I tried to get here as fast as I could."

Since I'm not one to look a gift horse in the mouth, I take my chances that she won't slap me and place a chaste kiss on her lips. I'm a guy and her lips feel like heavenly pillows...sue me.

She looks shocked for a second before quickly recovering. She smiles at me but there is a definite look of retribution in her eyes. Hmm, she's going to be fun, I muse.

"That's okay. As I was just *"trying"* - she grits out – to explain to Tommy, I was waiting on my boyfriend and didn't need any company." She gives me the brightest and fakest smile that I have ever seen.

I give him a nasty smirk. "Thanks for keeping my woman company. As you can see, I'm here now, so she no longer needs anyone to keep her company," I say while making sure that my hand is planted on her ass.

What? I have to make it look believable. No man in his right mind would give up touching an ass like hers if they were her man.

He looks between us and then to where my hand is strategically placed. "Right," he grunts. "Cool. See ya around." He frowns before turning and walking to some stupid looking, ridiculously raised truck. This dude is trying to compensate for the damage that those steroids have done, that's for damn sure.

Once he drives away, I feel a sharp little elbow smack into my ribs. I hiss out in pain. "Watch it, you little hellcat. You know I was just stabbed a few days ago. Aim higher if you must," I whine hoping for some sympathy.

The glare she's giving me says that won't be happening. "How about if I aim lower instead?" she drawls.

I narrow my eyes. "Now, is that any way to treat your handsome man? Especially after I was nice enough to come to your rescue? I could've left you with Tommy there?" I tilt my head in the direction that he drove away.

She huffs and crosses her arms over her ample chest. "You also stole a kiss and grabbed my ass. I'd say that you got something out of it."

I crush my hands to my heart pretending to be hurt. "Ouch, you wound me. I can't believe that you think that I wouldn't just help you out of the kindness of my heart."

She purses those lips that taste like chocolate and strawberries. "For some reason, you don't really strike me as the altruistic type."

I lean against the side of the building that we're standing in front of, thoroughly enjoying verbally sparring with her. "You don't know that. For all you know, I could be the next *Gandhi* or some shit."

The snort she makes is fucking adorable. She starts laughing and I just watch in pleasure the way her entire face lights up. "Right, because Gandhi would end a sentence with 'or some shit.' Yeah, you and he must be like distant cousins or something, huh?"

"You never know. I could be the nicest man that you'll ever meet. Obviously the most handsome." I ignore her eye roll at that one. "Hell, I could even be the man of your dreams."

See learning to watch people- thanks to my brother -has allowed me to pick up a few things. Like the fact that she looked away and blushes when I said I was the man of her dreams. Hmm, I guess I'm not the only one who's *"smitten"* as mom likes to say. This I can definitely work with.

"You are so far from a man that I would date." She chuckles but it sounds off.

I get up in her space a bit and see her eyes dilate. Jackpot! "And why's that *hellcat?*" I purr. "I'm sure that you and I could get along really well." I rub my nose against her cheek.

I listen as her breathing hitches for a second but she snaps out of it quickly...too quickly. "We would end up killing each other. And plus, I don't date players, been there and found the scumbag in my bed with my maid honor. I am done with men who are too full of themselves."

Well shit. Guess I now know why she and the doctor broke up. "That guy is a fucking moron," I tell her bluntly much to her apparent shock. "And just because I don't pretend to not realize what I look like, doesn't mean that I'm a player."

She raises a very well-manicured eyebrow at me. "Okay, then when was your last relationship?"

"A few years ago." She starts giving me a triumphant look that I'm going to try my best to squash. "But I was deployed for years, so it didn't make sense to force someone to put their life on hold for me."

"How long have you been out of the military?" she asks as she starts walking down the block and like a dutiful puppy, I follow after, barely keeping my tongue from lolling out of my mouth.

"Close to four years," I tell her honestly.

She stops to look through a window of a florist. "So, why haven't you dated anyone since?"

I scratch the back of my head, a move that she doesn't miss. "That's a little complicated," I hedge.

She looks around and her eyes light up when she spots the little mom and pop diner. "Well, come on," she says grabbing a hold of my arm and dragging me inside. "We can have some pie and coffee and you can tell me why it's so complicated that you've been single for so long."

We both take a seat at the old school counter and each order a slice of pie and a coffee. I ordered apple while she opted for pecan...I guess she couldn't be totally perfect.

Once we each get our coffees and she puts enough sugar to put someone into a diabetic coma into hers, she looks at me with raised eyebrows.

I sigh heavily. "Okay, but listen to me fully before passing judgment."

She gives me a wary look before taking a sip of her sugar...I mean coffee. "That's not really sounding too good already."

I hold up my hand and she just nods. I wait for the waitress to place our pies in front of us and leave before I start. "Okay, so when I first moved here, I had a thing for this woman named Erin, who's a bartender at Home Plate."

I take a bite of my pie and moan at how good it is. "What I didn't realize at first is that she's a lesbian."

Aimee chokes as she bites into her pie. I try to pat her on the back but she waves me off. "I'm okay." She puts her hand to her mouth and coughs. "I'm good. Keep going. You now have my full attention," she says through watery eyes.

After a few seconds, I give her a smirk. "I thought I might. Anyway, it didn't take me too long to figure out. But see the thing is, that I always go to the bar with my buddies from work including my brother."

She gives me a frown and I can't help but stare at how she licks her fork. She is so damn sexy and has no idea all the wicked thoughts that she's causing to run through my head with that pink tongue of hers. Jesus, I need to calm down before everyone in this diner gets a show.

She finishes licking every speck off that lucky fork. "Okay, what's the big deal with going with your friends?" she asks oblivious to my plight.

"I'm not always super quick on shit like that, especially if I like the woman. And of course, she flirts with male customers to make tips. But if I figured out that she was a lesbian, that means that at least a few of the other guys did as well."

"Okay?" she asks uncertainly.

"Those fuckers were content to watch me hit on someone who was never going to give me the time of day."

Aimee nods her head slowly before taking another bite. "Okay, I can see how you would be a little upset about that. But how does this affect why you've been single for so long?"

I give her my winning smile. "Ah, see Erin and I became good friends. Such good friends in fact that she mentioned how my traitorous buddies and brother have a bet going about how long it would take me to figure out that she bats for the other team. They all add in money each month that I haven't figured it out. I guess they each have a schedule for each week. So, whenever I "figure" it out, whoever has that week wins."

"Well, besides that being shitty of your friends, I don't get why you didn't call them out on it."

"Now where's the fun in that? Plus, I convinced Erin to get in on the bet. She and I have agreed to split the money. So, on her week, I'll let on that I know the truth and we pocket all of their money. And since it's been going on for so long, the jackpot is now up to like ten grand or something. It's definitely a nice chunk of change to have."

She blinks at me repeatedly. "That's actually really clever." I beam at the compliment. "But I still don't get why you stayed single."

"I wanted to see how heartless my friends and their wives truly are. I made it seem like I'm totally in love with her and that I'm convinced that one day she'll give me a shot. Not a single one of them has tried to warn me at all. But it would look bad if I was dating someone while pretending to be in love with Erin." I shrug and finish off my pie.

"Your friends sound kind of mean."

I give her a smile. "They're all actually really great and loyal." I hold my hand up when she raises an eyebrow in disbelief. "They would do anything for me. But we're a crazy bunch, especially when all together. There is nothing that we like more than getting a laugh. Even better if it's at one of our expenses. It's never malicious and never actually harmful."

"But they think that you like her."

I nod. "True. But since they know that she's a lesbian, they also know that none of our conversations would be in-depth enough for actual feelings."

She purses her lips. "I suppose. But it still sounds really mean."

"And that's the beauty of Erin and I playing this up. Not only do we get their money, but I get to make them feel really stupid. Win-win for me really, even if I did have to take a long hiatus from dating."

"I'll give it to you, you're definitely dedicated once you put your mind to something."

"You have no idea," I tell her with a wink. "So, how's Friday night?"

She looks perplexed. "For what?"

"Our date, of course."

"I am not going on a date with you," she argues.

"And why not?" I pretend to be offended, but truthfully, I didn't actually expect her to give in right away. She's stubborn and I, unfortunately, really like that quality in a woman.

"Because you still have bad idea/ heartbreak and weight gain written all over you. There is no way I'm going to put myself through that," she sighs.

I frown. "I was following you until the weight gain part."

"From eating ice cream because of a broken heart. Or brownies, I went through a lot of brownies," she says.

"You should take a chance."

She rolls her pretty eyes. "I already took a chance. I walked in on him having sex with my now ex-best friend. And worst is, I still have to see both of them all the time at work."

My eyes widen. "She works with you too?" Jesus, I can see why she's leery.

"Yeah," she drawls. "She was your nurse after I left."

I blink a few times. "That annoying bitch?" I ask shocked because damn, her ex really is a fucking moron. You do not give up quality like Aimee for a straight-up whore, I think to myself.

Aimee barks out a laugh and covers her mouth quickly while turning beet red. "Yep, that's her."

"Let me guess, the doctor that she ignored me almost the entire time I was there for, is your ex?" I knew that guy looked like a douchebag.

"Ding, ding, ding."

"You could do way better than him. Much better. You should be with someone who's handsome, funny, has sexy abs, and who could totally kick the shit out of that pansy-ass," I say as seriously as possible.

She gives me a smile while shaking her head. "You just don't quit, do you?"

"Not when I see something that I really want.," I tell her ominously.

She pats my arm and her touch feels electric. I know that she feels it too just from how her breathing hitched. But as soon as she has her reaction, she covers it. "I hate to break it to you, but I am one thing that you aren't going to get, no matter how determined you are." She gives me a sad little smile.

I just give her a smirk. "We'll see hellcat, we'll see."

"This is getting freaking ridiculous already!" I grumble as I spot Declan...yet again, for the third time this week.

I lost count last week after our *"pie date"* as he's taken to calling it. He is literally everywhere these days! It's like everywhere I turn...there he and his sexy self are. If I didn't know that he was a police officer, I would swear that he's some weirdo stalker.

Stacey looks at me with a frown. "I don't know why you have such a problem with seeing him. I really don't get why you won't go out with that man who has asked you out every single time that he's seen you. I would not be turning down a man that fine. If anything, I would be jumping in his arms and trying to keep other bitches far, far away."

"Then you date him," I growl and try to ignore the stab of jealousy that I feel when I imagine the two of them together.

She snorts none too delicately. "Honey, you'd have to be blind and just plain stupid to not realize that, that gorgeous specimen of beef only has eyes and other parts just for you."

I playfully roll my eyes at her but secretly enjoy hearing that. Who wouldn't? "I'm sure he's like this with every woman who turns him down. I'm sure that it's just a game to him." The words taste bitter on my tongue. I just don't know if it's because of the words themselves or because I don't believe them.

Stacey gives me an incredulous look. "Girl, please. That is not the type of man that a woman turns down. That is the type of man that other woman cut each other over." She holds out her arm. "Just take a look around, every woman in this place has their eyes on him."

I frown when I do as she says and see that, indeed, every woman and a few men in this place are drooling over him. "And this just proves my point. A man like him does not just stick to one woman. He is way too hot for that."

Stacey and I are at the local Mexican restaurant having dinner and drinks since we both have the whole weekend off. I pull a chip out of the basket and dip it into the salsa. I swear, I could totally make a meal out of just this appetizer. I take a bite and moan at the deliciousness of it.

"Who are all those people that he's with?" Stacey asks while slurping her margarita through her straw.

I look over and see that he is indeed with a huge group of people. But on second glance, I recognize all the guys from the night that he came in with the stab wound. Was it really only two weeks ago? It feels like so much longer.

"I think those are the guys that he works with and their wives," I say.

"Well, at least you know that he isn't stalking you. There is no way that he could get that many people in on it."

"Yeah, I guess." I frown and tilt my head at her. "But you don't think that it's just a little weird that he seems to be everywhere lately?" I fiddle with the straw of my drink.

Stacey gives me a contemplative look. She looks around the crowded restaurant and then back at me. "Yes and no. I mean we do live in a small town and you're bound to run into him. But I do think that whenever he sees you now, he makes sure that you notice him."

She does have a point. We really do live in a small town. I only moved here a few years ago after college, when I got the job working at the hospital. Even after only living here for such a short amount of time, I still know a ton of people in town. "You're right. I'm just being dumb. Plus, why would a guy like him stalk someone like me." I snort and eat another chip.

Stacey sighs. "I hate what that break-up did to you. You are beyond gorgeous with a body that most women would kill to have. Add in the fact that you're smart, caring, sweet – when you want to be – a great cook and an all-around awesome human being, and you're pretty much the total package."

I laugh and raise my eyebrow. "Pretty much?"

She nods her head saucily. "You would be the total package but you can't clean to save your life. Poor Brad bitches about your housekeeping skills all the time."

As much as I would love to defend myself, I just can't. I really do suck at housework. I don't know what it is, but I will wait until the place is just gross before I clean it. I make sure that the kitchen is always spotless, but other than that, I'm a disaster.

"Whatever," I mumble for a lack of anything better to say.

Stacey just shakes her head and grabs a chip. I take a sip of my drink and promptly choke on it when I hear the voice above us.

"Well, it's good to know that I'll be doing all the cleaning," Declan drawls from his spot next to our table.

Stacey starts laughing as I choke and try not to die from the margarita I'm sipping on. Although, it's probably not the worst way to go.

Declan pats my back and frowns. "I've had to do this to you before. I'm beginning to get concerned that you aren't able to feed yourself properly."

While his voice sounds ever-so concerned, his dark eyes are dancing with nothing but mirth. I slap away his hand and pull myself together.

"I blame you. It only happens when you're around. Did anyone ever tell you that you might be a curse and not a blessing?" I say breathlessly and I swear it's not from his proximity. That's a lie, the voice in my head says but no one needs to know the truth.

I look over when I hear a bunch of laughs and realize that he and his friends have been seated right next to us. How the hell is it possible for their

34

large group to be seated next to us. I see the waitress pushing tables together. I just cannot believe the luck.

"She's spunky, I like it," says a very pretty brunette, attached to the giant one's side. With their size difference, you would think that they would look weird, but they look adorable together. "Loki, you better watch out with this one."

I smile and then frown at Declan. "Loki?" I ask with raised eyebrows.

He gives the brunette a dirty look that everyone laughs at. "It's nothing. Just Kayla being salty."

The brunette that I'm guessing is Kayla smirks and laughs at him. "Oh, it was most definitely me being *salty*, but that's only after Declan was being annoying."

I look at her. "Him...annoying? I can't imagine that," I deadpan, getting a chuckle out of everyone but Declan. I'm pretty sure that I even caught his stoic twin smirking. "But why call him Loki? Have you seen that guy, he's hot," I say without thinking.

"What's that supposed to mean, hellcat?" Declan asks with a put-out look on his face. Geez, men and their fragile egos.

I blink innocently at him. "Don't try to change the subject. I'm asking Kayla why she calls you Loki." I swiftly deflect like a damn boss.

Kayla gives me a smile that tells me she knows damn well why I did that but will help me out. "I call him Loki because when I met him, I didn't know his name but I knew Damon's. And since he was so annoying, I decided that he was like the character Loki...the brother that no one likes." She smiles sweetly at Declan who's glaring at her.

"You still could've given me something more badass. You know that reflects my true awesomeness," he pouts.

She grins evilly at him and then looks at me quickly. "Well, how was I supposed to know that you would eventually dress up as an ugly hooker?"

Stacey spits out her drink, luckily away from me and everyone else. I'm just sitting here blinking rapidly at him. Stacey and I look at each other and then back at him. He's getting so red that I'm afraid he's going to explode.

"I didn't really peg you as a crossdresser. And why an ugly hooker? You should try pageant queen," Stacey says completely seriously much to everyone's amusement.

I love her, I truly do. But some days her brain and her mouth really don't connect well...or at all. While everyone else is sitting in their chairs laughing, Declan is still standing beside us. He's looking at her like he can't figure out how she meant it. When she looks at him and tilts her head seriously, I can tell that he realizes that she was serious and not being a shit.

Declan rubs his eyebrow and stares at her. "Do I really look like a crossdresser to you?" he asks earnestly. No one is even trying to hide their snickers...me included.

She looks him over and shrugs. "I didn't think one of my boyfriends that I lived with for two years was gay until I came home to him cuddled on our couch with another guy." Everyone is just staring at her with their mouths open while she calmly sips her drink.

"Wow, you must hate him," a blonde woman who resembles a pin-up says.

Stacey smiles at her and shakes her head. "No, not at all. He was still in the closet because his parents suck and he was afraid that they would refuse to have anything to do with him. Which they did when they found out, after calling him a bunch of horrible things," she says with a nasty look on her face but then shakes her head. "I don't blame him and totally get why he was living a double life. We're still the best of friends. He's actually Aimee's roommate now. The three of us are together pretty much non-stop since we all work together as well."

Crickets are all you hear. Well, not really since it's Friday night in one of the town's most favorite restaurants, but you get the picture.

"I guess we're adding two more to the group...most likely three," the guy with hazel eyes says.

Stacey and I look at each other in confusion and then back at the man. He just gives us a bright smile. "I'm Rocco...welcome to the family."

And that was how we ended up pushing our table together with theirs and spending the rest of the evening being thoroughly entertained.

What's not entertaining is the fact that I'm pretty sure that I am dying this morning. The other women were really bad influences. I swear our table seemed to have never-ending pitchers of margaritas. A tequila hangover is a bitch.

I mentally go through what I have to do today, to see if I can just stay in bed and die for the day. And as luck would have it, I was smart enough to know that I wouldn't stop at one, okay two, - who really only drinks one margarita – drinks and made sure that my schedule was clear.

I burrow deeper into my pillow and blankets and try to figure out a way to convince Brad to take care of me. I hear another male voice besides Brad's out in the living room or kitchen. Damn, he must've gotten lucky last night. Well, at least one of us is getting some.

But the more that I hear the voice, the more that something seems to be clawing at the back of my mind. My mind that is still in a tequila-fueled haze and won't be clearing up anytime soon.

I grumble and throw my blankets over my head, trying to block out any and all sound. Even the voices, a few rooms away are too much for my fragile brain right now. Never again am I drinking margaritas...at least until I forget how bad this hangover is.

I hear my bedroom door open and then close and I hiss at the sound. "Please Brad, be quiet," I whine. "I'm pretty sure that I'm dying and my head will explode if you make too much noise."

"I tried to tell you not to have those last four drinks," an amused voice drawls. A deep sexy voice that I hear in my dreams, a voice that most certainly does not belong to Brad.

I sit straight up and immediately regret it when the whole world starts to spin. "Oh my god," I moan, as I grab my head so that it doesn't fall off. I peak out of one eye and yup, definitely not Brad. "What are you doing here Declan?"

"Well good morning to you too hellcat. Or should I call you wildcat after last night?" He smirks down at me with a raised eyebrow.

My eyes get as huge as saucers. "Tell me that we didn't!" I stutter. "Please tell me that we didn't have sex?" I toss the covers off frantically and see that I'm fully dressed in sweat pants and a long sleeve shirt. I release a huge sigh. That would've been so bad.

Declan is leaning against my door with his arms crossed over his chest with a large frown on his handsome face. "Ya know, that's not usually the reaction I get when a woman finds me at her place in the morning."

I stare up at him. "What is the reaction? Throwing things to make you leave, because I could totally do that," I tell him sweetly.

His eyes turn into slits. "You should be super nice to me right now. Especially after I drove your drunk ass home and stayed when you begged me not to leave. I even cuddled just like you wanted."

"I did not!" I gasp horrified.

His smirk does nothing to make me feel better. "Oh, yes you did. And that was only after you tried to molest me during the ride home. I thought that I was going to have to tie your hands together to stop you from doing your best impression of an octopus. Hellcat is most definitely the best nickname for you."

I can't believe it. "But we didn't...you know...right?" I ask hopefully.

"You couldn't even walk, I had to carry you up here? What do you think?" he drawls.

I crash back into my pillows saying a silent thank you as well as a please kill me now. "I actually did and said all of that?" I cover my face with my hands.

"Mm-hmm. It was pretty entertaining...well until I started driving. It's very distracting to have a woman rubbing her hands up and down your stomach, or as you were calling it, my washboard." I can hear the mirth in his voice.

Covering my face with my hands, I peek out of the cracks between my fingers. "Did I do anything embarrassing in front of everyone else?"

His lips twitch. "No, you were actually the best-behaved drunk woman out of the group of you. Although that's not really saying too much, considering you were all sloshed."

"Oh thank God! You, I can handle, everyone else and I would've been finding the nearest bridge to jump off of."

"Didn't picture you for the suicidal type."

I look up at him. How can one man look so damn good leaning against a door, even in the clothes that he was wearing the night before? "Actually, I'm not. I'm also terrified of heights, so I probably wouldn't even be able to get very far before chickening out," I huff.

"Good to know," he states, but I'm just not sure to what part.

I look around my room nervously, making sure that I haven't left out anything embarrassing. "So, umm, not that I'm not grateful and everything, but what are you still doing here?"

He walks over and hands me a cup of coffee and some pain meds that I didn't see until just now. I take them and give him a grateful smile. "Well, I'm just waiting for you to get on your feet and then we can go back to my place so that I can change."

I blink repeatedly over the rim of the glorious elixir that will hopefully bring me back to life. "Say what now?"

Oh, I so don't like the grin he's giving me. It's part sweet little boy and part sexy man who is up to no good. And my damn body really needs to stop reacting to his presence. Stupid good looking, sweet jerk just has to smell incredible too. Who smells good the next morning before a shower? He's a damn warlock or something, I just know it!

"Well, we made an agreement. I would stay and *cuddle with you*, - he says with a wicked smile – and you would spend the whole day with me. Our second date if you will."

I flounder around for a minute trying to think of something to say to get me out of this. I will never survive a whole day with just him. I'm a strong woman, but I'm not that strong. "You..I was drunk! You can't take what a drunk woman says to heart. I was feeling absolutely no pain. There is no way that I'm moving out of this bed today, especially when I don't remember making this agreement," I huff triumphantly. "And we are not dating!" I say for good measure.

"Huh? And here I thought that you were a woman of your word."

"I am," I growl. "I've told you plenty of times that we're not dating and I mean it. See, I'm a woman of my word." I cross my arms.

He sits down next to me and I swear that the pheromones that he gives off are nothing short of pure sin. He smells like the most decadent chocolate cake that I want to take a huge bite out of. Dammit, now I want him and chocolate cake.

He leans in close and I can feel his breath across my face. It's weird, I don't generally enjoy someone being all up in my space, but for some reason, I want him even closer. I unconsciously lean forward to get closer to him. We're now mere centimeters apart, our noses almost touching.

"Aims, we are spending the day together and it will be considered our second date. And then after that, we'll have a third and so on. Now, you can either get your fine ass out of bed and into the shower all by yourself. Or I'm going to drag you out of bed and help you shower. Trust me when I say, that I would really enjoy option number two, so please be my guest and be as stubborn as you want."

I narrow my eyes at the sexy jackass. "You do realize that my roommate is out there. I can yell for help and tell him to call the police to come and get your annoying ass out of here," I snip.

His lips twitch, causing me to just get angrier for some reason. "You could if he wasn't one hundred percent on board with us dating. Apparently, he hated your ex and really likes me and my determination. So, call for help all you want. But one way or another, we will be spending the entire day together. So, make your choice hellcat, option one or two?"

Asshole!

SAPD SWAT

Declan

I can feel the daggers that she's shooting at me still and I can't honestly say that I blame her too much. Unfortunately for me, she chose option one after a minute of grumbling and calling me an asshole under her breath. I like that she was pissed and still tried not to hurt my feelings with cursing me out to my face. I know, I know, probably not what she meant, but let me just have my little fantasy.

We've just left my place and I could tell that she was beyond surprised. I'm guessing she thought that I lived in some disgusting bachelor pad, instead of a clean and well-decorated little three-bedroom ranch house. The look on her face when we pulled into my driveway said it all.

The fact that she walked around with her mouth open when we went inside was an extremely satisfying reaction. Most people assume that I would be a slob or whatever just because I'm a single guy.

However, mom was determined that Damon and I would be able to keep a clean home, that she decorated. I wasn't going that far. Thanks to my mother being on us for years, Damon and I are almost compulsive about keeping our space clean. I have to say, it was very helpful already being trained for that when we went into the military.

Mom actually tried to make sure that we could cook as well. She didn't want us going to our future wives like dad had come to her...helpless. Grandma babied dad and mom paid the price, or so she complains. She gave up with the cooking thing after the third or fourth fire that Dam and I started. She figured as long as we could clean and do laundry, it would be okay.

So, yeah, the look of utter disbelief on Aimee's face when she walked in was pretty damn funny. I like keeping people on their toes and seeing their genuine reactions to things. When you catch someone off guard, that's usually when you see the most truth. I'm not overly cynical like my twin but face it, a lot of people suck ass.

I left her to snoop around while I showered and got ready. I enjoyed the fact that she didn't even look slightly embarrassed to be caught looking through my cabinets. Her response? "I need to make sure that you're not some stalkerish serial killer." I may have replied no to only the serial killer part, but she doesn't really need to know that.

Now here we sit in my truck, on our way to go have some lunch, since her ass didn't wake up until after ten this morning. She's got her arms crossed over her wonderfully ample chest and is glaring at me. I guess someone doesn't like losing. I mentally shrug. Oh well, her loss is my gain.

"Why are you smirking?" she growls adorably at me...tiny little hellcat.

I look to my right and flash her my best smile. "I'm just so happy getting to spend the whole day with you, that I can't keep the smile off of my face."

Her eyes close slightly and she purses her lips. "You do realize that after today is over, I am making sure that you are never near me again...right?"

Such a stubborn ass. We both know that she likes me, maybe not as much as I like her – I have been technically stalking the poor woman for a few weeks – but she likes me and it irks her. She just refuses to give into this thing between us on principle alone. I have never met anyone as stubborn. I'm so excited to get her to give in.

"I can guarantee that after today, you'll be begging me to stay with you forever."

43

She raises an eyebrow and gets that look on her face that I've come to learn means that she's about to be a smartass. "As what? A ghost? Because you're going to die *"accidentally"* at some point today."

My lips twitch involuntarily. I'll give it to her...she's a lot of fun to spar with. "You know, most of the wives in the group have threatened to kill us at one time or another."

"I can't imagine why," she murmurs, which I ignore.

"And they're all happily married. It gives me a lot of hope for our future."

She's now frowning at me. "Do you have a mental illness? You get that normal people don't say that to a woman that they've basically kidnapped right? Should you call a psychiatrist and maybe get some medicine?" She gnaws at her bottom lip.

It's now my turn to frown at her. "I don't have any mental illness."

She gives me a dubious look. "Are you sure?" She raises her hands when I glare at her. "Hey, there's nothing wrong with it. A lot of people have some sort of mental disorder these days. It's nothing to be ashamed of. I'm just checking to see if you need to be on the proper medication...that's all.

"I don't have any mental disorders," I growl growing agitated.

She turns her head towards her window. "If you say so," she mutters.

This stubborn ass woman. "Can we please just enjoy lunch and get to know each other a little better?" I ask as I pull into the parking lot.

She gives me a saucy smile. "Sure thing, you're the one running this kidnapping, I mean day after all." She hops out before I can say anything.

Did I think that she would give in easily? No, a man can hope but she's determined to stay single and I'm guessing that it has to do with her ex. I'm way too awesome for her to just not like me. But damn, this woman is infuriating and as stubborn as a damn mule. I just have to channel my inner Damon...that's all. I need to somehow find all the patience in the world.

I quickly follow her and make it to the door just in time to open it for her. She gives me a smirk and a wink. "Thanks," she says as she pats my stomach before sashaying her ass right past me.

When we get to the hostess booth, she looks like she saw something that she wants to squash. I look in the direction that she's now glaring and see the doctor and my nurse from the hospital. Ah, the ex and the chick he cheated on her with. For the love of God, can't I catch a break with this woman? All I wanted was a nice lunch, a few laughs, her to realize how amazing I am and then for her to agree to be mine...forever preferably.

I run my hands up her arms and feel her shiver in response, making me smile inwardly. "Do you want to go somewhere else?"

She looks up at me with the first genuine smile she's given me all day. "No, that's okay. I'm used to having to deal with them. Plus, I really like the BLT's here."

I bend down and look her in the eyes. "If you're sure?"

She reaches up on the tippy toes and gives me a kiss on the cheek. "I'm sure. Let's not let them ruin your well-planned kidnapping."

I give her a blank

She blinks up at me innocently and shrugs. "I saw my opportunity and I took it. Sue me."

I just shake my head and smile. I look at the teenage hostess and smile. "Two please."

She gives us a smile and grabs two menus. "Sure, follow me."

She leads us through the rows of tables and right past Aims' ex. My girl just walks right past him like he's nothing. Out of the corner of my eye, I can see him look at me with surprise. Yeah, fucker, she's moved on, my mind screams. Okay, not really, but he doesn't need to know that. I give him an obnoxious smirk and wink as I walk past. I've never stated that I was the good twin. Everyone just automatically assumes that I am after meeting Damon.

We both take our seats and I make sure that I'm seated with the wall to my back. I have a view of the entire restaurant, including her ex and his chick, who keep looking over at us.

"Your waitress will be right with you," the hostess says as she hands us our menus and then promptly leaves.

"We appear to have an audience," I state lowly while looking over my menu, even though I already know what I'm getting. I don't deviate very often.

Aimee rolls her pretty eyes. "I don't see why. Neither of them gave a damn about me when they were a part of my life. They really shouldn't care now that they're no longer part of it," she says simply like it doesn't even bother her anymore. Too bad her aversion to dating me proves otherwise.

"It still must be tough to have to see them all of the time," I say before our waitress comes over and introduces herself.

Since we both seem to know what we want, we both order quickly, much to the waitress' appreciation. She gives us a smile and leaves just as quickly as she appeared.

Aimee gives me a cute, thoughtful little frown. "I wouldn't say that it's tough. It's more annoying than anything else these days. I no longer care that they're together. It's just how they went about it that really chaps my ass, I guess. He could've simply just ended things between us and then started dating her. But either way, I'm glad that they showed their true colors and that I'm rid of them. I have no need for people like that in my life." She looks up at me with imploring eyes. "It just...stings...ya know?"

I nod my head. "Yeah, I do, I get it. No one should be betrayed by the people that they think they can count on the most. It takes away a lot of trust that you have in general. No one deserves to be hurt like that."

She gives me a grateful smile. "Yeah, pretty much."

"So," I start wanting to change the subject to something more upbeat. "What do you want to do for the rest of the day?"

She raises an eyebrow at me in question. "You're asking me?" She chuckles incredulously. "You're the one who kidnapped me from my nice, warm, cozy bed and you're saying that you don't have a plan."

I toy with my straw and give her a smile. "Oh hellcat, one thing that you should learn quickly, is that I always have a plan. No, I was just trying to be nice by letting you pick what you would like to do. I'm an incredibly thoughtful guy like that."

"I would like to still be in my bed, sleeping off the tequila," she says with a serious face.

"Now, now, we did that last night. Today is my turn."

She places her elbows on the table and leans forward. "See, I really don't think that I agreed to anything last night and that you're just making this shit up."

I lean forward and get nose to nose. "Trust me Aims, you were ready to agree to anything last night, as long as I cuddled with you." I snap my fingers. "Also, as long as you could touch my washboard." I grin at how red her face is turning.

"Will you stop saying that?" she hisses.

I scoff. "Are you kidding me? That's all I'm going to call my abs from now on. I'll forever ask you if you would like to pet my washboard." I nod my head with a smirk as she starts glaring at me again. "Yeah, that sounds like a mixture of clean and dirty...I like it."

She purses her plump lips and frowns at me with her arms crossed. "Whatever," she mumbles before she looks at me. "It doesn't matter anyway because once you drop me off home, I am staying as far away from you as possible."

"Challenge accepted," I reply.

Her eyes turn into little slits. "This is not a game or a challenge Declan," she growls in her tiny, sweet voice. It's completely ineffective but extremely endearing all the same. "You have bad news bears written all over you. I do not need any more pain and anguish in my life, thank you very much," she huffs.

I blink a few times before I reply. "First off," I hold up my index finger, "what are you, like sixty? That show was on when our parents were kids." She just rolls her eyes as I continue. "Second, I am one of the best guys in the world, just ask my mama and sister-in-law. Hell, ask any one of the wives." I rub my chin thoughtfully. "Except maybe Kayla, her salty ass would say bad things about me just to be a shithead. But everyone else, feel free to ask them how awesome I am."

"You don't have any self-confidence issues, do you?" she drawls.

I chuckle. "Have you met and seen me? Why would I?"

She has that look in her eyes again that says she's about to come back at me with something really good. I wonder what it says about me that I love when she's all feisty and growly? Not that I really give a fuck...but still. I probably do have a few issues that I won't be addressing anytime soon...or ever. Either or. But just as she opens her mouth to speak, we hear an annoying ass voice that I could've done without ever hearing again. Just when I'm making some damn headway. I'm beginning to see why Dam really wouldn't mind offing a few people.

"You finally found someone, good for you," The whoreish other nurse says in the most condescending tone that I've ever heard.

It takes every ounce of will power that I have to just sit here and remain calm. I would never hit a woman but I'm not above tripping this bitch, possibly into traffic. Jesus, people are right, we are the world's worst cops.

Aimee looks up and gives her a saccharine smile. "I did. Luckily for me, Declan doesn't like cheap whores, so I see this going well. Not that I have to worry since I rid myself of any and all the day that I kicked you two out of my apartment," she says so sweetly, I'm likely to get a toothache.

The scowl that comes over this chick's face is hysterical. Damn, where is Marc and his fucking camera when you really need him? What is it that the girls would call someone like this chick? I start drumming my fingers on the table while I think. Ah-ha! Whorie…Barbie's whoreish cousin!

Whorie, as she will now forever be called, is glaring at Aimee with her hands on her bony hips. Jesus, I'm surprised that she doesn't puncture her hands, they're so pointy. What the hell does this fool grab onto from behind? I then look over at him and realize that he's probably a missionary, wham, bam, two-second man.

"I am not a whore." she hisses like a snake.

Aimee gets an evil smirk on her face. "Oh really? Because if you ask anyone else, a woman who sleeps with her friend's fiancée is most definitely a whore…a skanky one at that," Aimee slyly states right before taking a sip of her drink like she doesn't have a care in the world.

"Well maybe if you could keep Aaron satisfied, he wouldn't have come to me," Whorie says smugly. Must remain calm, must remain calm.

Aimee snorts. "Please, you now know damn well that it isn't very hard to please someone for two minutes." I knew it!

The jackass who was just standing there with an obnoxious grin is now as red as a tomato. I guess they shouldn't have tried to come and embarrass my woman - yeah, yeah, it counts if she will be in the future - in a quiet restaurant, voices carry. God, how the hell does Damon keep a straight face all of the time? I am dying here!

Stupid sputters. "I last much, much longer than that. I can go for hours if I want to."

Everyone looks at him incredulously before Whorie starts in again. "Whatever, at least I'm marrying a surgeon while you're what? Dating a guy who makes like thirty grand a year?" Her and stupid - he has to be to choose this bitch over Aimee - start snickering to each other.

I blink at them and try to contain my rage but it's tough. The only thing that's slightly helping is how pissed off Aimee looks. Yeah, she's definitely looking like a little hellcat right now. "Who cares how much he makes? At least

I know that if we get married, I'll never have to wonder who else he's sticking his dick into, unlike you."

And this just settled it. I am marrying her fine ass, hopefully sooner rather than later.

I just give them my best Damon smile. You know that one that suggests I might be part serial killer? Yeah, it's definitely creeping them out, I chuckle inwardly. "Oh, don't worry about how much I make Aims, that really has nothing to do with my net worth," I reply calmly before taking a sip of my drink.

They don't know that Damon and I come from old money. Like very old money. How no one figured it out when Damon was able to plan a getaway in a few days with no expenses spared should've clued some people in. It may have been a cabin in the woods, but it was the mansion of cabins. Our great-grandfather hit it big in the oil industry or whatever. Needless to say, I could sit on my ass for the rest of my life and still be able to send my kids to Harvard. Our parents raised us not to view money as too important, which is why Dam and I like making our own. But damn does it feel great in times like these.

"What are you talking about?" Stupid sneers.

I give him a triumphant grin. "My last name is DeWitt, as in Dewitt oil. Ringing any bells?" I smile smugly as they gape at me. Truthfully, I'm not liking the wary look in Aimee's eyes, but there's nothing that can be done about it right this moment.

"But that means that you're a...a," he stutters.

I nod my head solemnly. "A millionaire? Yes, it's an extremely difficult life being me, but I guess someone has to do it." I shrug. I'm such an asshole...and I love every second of it.

"Why would someone like you ever go near her?" the bitch spits out with nothing but venom. And I'm done.

"Probably because I like my women gorgeous, with curves and brains, instead of a bimbo waif. Now, I'm going to have to ask you to go back to your own table before I have the owner escort you out." My tone leaves no room for argument and these two finally seem to catch on that they no longer have the upper hand.

"Whatever," is huffed and they both turn and walk away quickly.

I look over at Aimee and get an uneasy feeling at the look that she's currently giving me. She opens her mouth a few times to speak but no words seem to come out. So I just sit here and wait, knowing that I have to let her say or ask whatever questions that she wants. It's not very often that my money comes up. Never really. Damon and I have never been ones to live extravagantly, actually no one in our family does. Well, except Grams, but she has some weird-ass obsession with tiny dogs that are expensive as hell. Annoying fluffy little ankle-biters.

"So, you're that DeWitt," she says in an almost robotic tone.

I scratch the back of my neck and thank God that the waitress has chosen this moment to bring our food. Not that I'm really hungry any longer. I lost my appetite when those two walked over and judging by the way that Aimee is eying her BLT, I'm guessing it was the same for her. Or my admission did, but I'm just going to tell myself that it was dumb and dumber.

Once the waitress leaves, we both just stare at each other. I look down and pick up a fry from my plate, mainly just so that I have something to do. I knew that I probably should have kept my mouth shut, but damn that bitch struck a nerve.

Aimee is playing with her bread with a serious look on her beautiful face. A look that doesn't really bode too well for me. "You're rich? Like crazy rich, and you're a SWAT officer who gets stabbed because he doesn't want anyone else to?"

"Ah…" I'm not really sure how she went from my money to me getting stabbed. "Yes?" I ask. I'm not too sure how she would like me to respond.

"Yeah, we are definitely not dating each other."

I narrow my eyes. "And why the hell not?" I growl, sounding more like my brother than myself. "Just because I have some money? That's kind of shitty don't you think? You don't even know me."

"Are you kidding me?" She leans in and hisses. "A little money? You're like fucking Scrooge McDuck or something. And it's not shitty. I was cheated on by that pathetic sack of shit over there and he isn't even a quarter of the perfection that you are. Heather's right about one thing, a guy like you can do a hell of a lot better than a girl like me."

"You're fucking serious right now?" I ask incredulously. "You're really going to throw away a chance at being with me and seeing where it goes because you're scared? That's a sad way to live your life, Aimee."

The look she gives me is pure menace. "It's not sad to want to protect yourself, Declan. It's human nature to want to keep pain away. Why would I want to open myself up to any of that, especially with a man who could literally get any woman he wants," she huffs out before shoving her plate of uneaten food away.

I give her a humorless laugh. "That's the thing Aimee, you're the only one that I want."

She gives me the saddest smile that I've ever seen. "For now."

It's been nine days since that awful lunch with Declan, not that I'm counting or anything. Nine days and I haven't seen him around anywhere. Which is completely what I wanted of course. I'm just making an observation that it's weird that I went from seeing him everywhere to him disappearing like a puff of smoke.

Okay, not really. He drove me home, it was the quietest and most awkward car ride ever, made sure that I made it to my door safely and then left without another word. Which is without a doubt, exactly what I wanted. Now if my stomach would just stop churning, that would be great. And it's not like I can actually miss someone who wasn't even a part of my life, no matter how many people wish that he was.

Lord, the earful that I got from Brad and Stacey that night was absolutely ridiculous. You would think that Declan had magical powers and charmed their asses into liking him. After yelling at me and telling me what a colossal moron I was for pushing a man like him away, they gave me the silent treatment for the rest of the night. Which kind of sucked considering I replayed the entire day over and over again, without having anyone to talk to.

I shake my head to try to dislodge all thoughts of that sexy as sin man. He's the type of man that can break you into a million pieces and I just don't have enough glue left anymore.

I sigh as I walk the aisles of the farmers market. I'm beyond exhausted from working my three days in a row and really should've just stayed home and in bed. Unfortunately, Brad also has the day off and I just couldn't deal with any more of his disapproving looks.

So here I am walking around aimlessly and just throwing random things into my cart. Though, this is all stuff that I'm sure I'll need. I've been meaning to try a few new recipes out anyway. I pick up a package of farmers cheese and look it over. I have had a craving for sweet cheese pierogis lately and the only way to get them is to make them myself or drive the two hours to my parents' house. I sigh again while staring at the cheese. Do I really want to do all of that work?

And it is a shit ton of work. Everything has to be made from scratch. It takes forever and a year to roll out the damn dough and cut it into circles. I'm not even going to get into how freaking tedious it is to stuff those suckers, close them up and then boil them before sautéing them. This will probably take me at least three hours. I snort to myself. It's not like I have anything better to do since I pushed an incredibly handsome, sweet and funny man away.

I toss the cheese into my cart and start to push it before I stop dead in my tracks. In front of my cart is Declan. I just stand there holding onto the handle of my cart and realize that it isn't Declan, it's Damon. I swear, he just really gives off a weird vibe. How two men can look identical and still be so easy to identify is incredible.

I frown at the mirror image of the man that I most certainly do not miss. Nope, not at all. "Damon."

Mister personality tilts his head at me but says nothing. He's literally standing in front of my cart with his massive arms crossed. And if that isn't intimidating enough, he's wearing a black T-shirt that looks like it's about to split right down the middle, worn-in jeans and black boots. With his tattoos and general demeanor, people are giving us a wide berth. Glad to know someone would actually come to my rescue if he was actually a threat, I think sarcastically.

I start chuckling to myself causing him to give me a wary look. Yeah, that makes two of us, pal. I start to push the cart again because standing in the middle of the aisle staring at each other is just plain creepy. Luckily, he gets the clue and moves alongside of me. Oh yay, he didn't just happen to step in front of my cart accidentally.

Knowing that he most likely won't go away without some prompting I decided to give in. "What's up Damon? I highly doubt that you're here for a social visit."

He looks down at me with a blank expression. "You ain't dumb. You know why I'm here."

I roll my eyes and keep walking knowing damn well that I'm not going to shake him. "Yes, I'm not stupid, I know that it's because of Declan, but what is it exactly that you want. As much fun as you are to be around" - I ignore the twitch in his eye – "I would prefer if you would just get straight to the point. I didn't peg you for a guy who makes idle chit chat," I say drolly.

I'm pretty sure that I see his lip twitch but I'm not really sure. The fluorescent lighting in here is dreadful. "Ya know, most people don't talk to me that way."

I shrug while looking at the avocados. Just this morning on Pinterest, I found a recipe for a shrimp and avocado pocket bread thing. Okay, it doesn't sound great, but the video made it look yummy. Plus, I just added a ton of shrimp since it is on sale. "I'm sure that you freak most people out."

"Not you." A statement, not a question.

I look over my shoulder at him. "No, not me. Even after what happened between Declan and me at lunch," - I can't help but wrinkle my nose - "you still wouldn't hurt me. I would have to do something truly horrible. Most people go by looks alone when it comes to fear. Plus, we both know that you could be far more intimidating than you're currently being. So, no…not me."

He makes a weird non-committal sound that I have a feeling is a part of his regular vocabulary. He picks out a few perfect avocados and hands them to me. His lips definitely twitch when my eyebrows automatically go up in shock. "You get good at certain things when your wife is pregnant and wants nothing but avocados."

I turn back around so that he doesn't see my smile. Yeah, he can definitely freak a person out a bit but not when he talks about learning how to pick out the perfect avocado for his wife. I'm a hundred percent sure that he would not appreciate me telling him how adorable that I think it is though.

"Was it the money or something else that scared you off?" he asks after following me down another aisle. Admittedly, it's kind of handy having him around on a Saturday afternoon. People are literally getting out of my way as fast as humanly possible.

I look over at him with a scowl before turning back to grab a few lemons. "It's not the money, though that is a bit intimidating." I look at him again and he just nods. "Honestly, I just don't want to get hurt again. Sure, it might be lonely, but it's safe. And Declan, he's anything but safe."

"He would never hurt you," Damon growls menacingly. "He would never hurt a woman."

I can't help my smirk. It's funny how someone so stoic can get all wound up for certain people. I pat him on one of his gigantic arms. "I didn't mean it like that, oh friendly one. I was talking about my heart. Your brother could shatter me and I really don't think that I could come back from that. So, yes, I'm playing it safe."

He looks a little less serial killerish after my statement. Seriously, how is his wife like the sweetest and most outgoing woman that I've met? Opposites must really attract. "And you don't think that he's worth the risk."

"I didn't say that," I huff with my arms crossed against my chest, mirroring the ginormous pain in my ass standing across from me.

He lifts one shoulder that could probably hold a small car. "Didn't have to, your actions speak for you."

I grit my teeth and decide the best course of action is just to continue shopping. The last thing I need to do is get into a yelling match with him.

Granted, I'd most likely be the only one yelling, but whatever. Pushing my cart down the aisle, I can feel his eyes burning a hole through my back. "What do you want from me? What did you actually hope to accomplish from this little visit?"

"I wanted to see what about you was so special. Why you not wanting to give him a chance has him miserable. Why he hasn't actually smiled since the day you two had lunch together. I'm just trying to understand what about you has him so torn up."

I feel like he literally just punched me in the stomach. The worst part isn't even how he said it. He didn't say it with any sort venom. He's actually just curious and wanted to figure it out. No, why I feel like I can't breathe has entirely to do with what he said. I can't believe that Declan is actually this upset about me not agreeing to go out with him. A man who could get any woman with the snap of his fingers does not get broken up over a fairly average woman like me.

I swear that I'm not putting myself down. I just happen to be realistic. Am I going to be modeling anytime soon? No...fuck no. Am I pretty? Sure, in the girl next door, average sort of way. And that's the thing, guys who look like a living and breathing Greek statue, don't get all mopey over the girl next door, they just don't. But dammit, there is no deceit in Damon's eyes. I asked him a question and the life of the party here answered it.

"That was never my intention," I say in a small voice while not being able to meet his piercing eyes.

"No, maybe not, but you did all the same," he says calmly.

"Well, what's done is done."

He makes another one of those grunt sounds. Seriously, what the hell are those supposed to mean? Yes? No? I'm going to kill you and devour your soul?

I'm buying this guy a dictionary and a thesaurus, just to help out the rest of humanity.

"That's a lot of food that you have in your cart there."

I look down and see that it is indeed pretty full. Huh? When did that happen? Oh, well, not like it will go to waste. "I like to cook."

He gives me a look that I just can't place. If I'm being truthful, I'm not certain that I want to either. "That's funny."

I give him a dubious look. I know that I'm walking right into his trap but I just can't help myself. "What's funny?"

He shrugs before turning around. "Declan likes to eat," he calls over his shoulder before flicking two fingers in my direction, which I'm guessing is his way of saying goodbye? Such a weird guy.

Well shit, now what should I do?

Two hours later:

I'm pacing around my kitchen with the time bomb, my phone, in my hand. For the life of me, I just can't press the green little send button. I'm not entirely sure why I feel so much trepidation about making this phone call. Well, that's not completely true either.

If I make this phone call, things can go either two ways. The first is Declan and I dating, getting married and having adorable babies. The second is we date, I fall head over heels for him and he completely shatters me, mind, body, and soul.

So, yeah, I know damn well why my finger seems to only hover above the screen and not actually touch it. Either way you look at it, both of the scenarios are scary in their own right. I just really need to figure out which one scares me the most.

"For the love of all that's holy, just press that damn button girl and get on with it already," Brad whines at a pitch that would make dogs howl. "I am not getting any younger here, and neither are you," he says with a saucy smirk that I want to whack off of his face.

"I'm still thinking," I huff as I continue my useless pacing.

As I walk past the island again, Brad swipes my phone out of my hand. I try but fail to hold onto it. I glare at the traitor. "Don't even think about it," I growl, still trying to reach over the island and grab it back from him.

He lifts it in the air and gives me a half smug, half innocent smirk. "Do what?" He blinks his ridiculously long eyelashes. Seriously, why is that men always have the best damn eyelashes? "This?" he asks as I see him hit the call button.

"No!" I shriek and try to get to it in time to no avail. Brad tosses me the phone and starts walking down the hall towards his room while I stare at the thing in horror.

"Hello?" I hear that sexy deep voice that I haven't heard in what feels like forever.

I sigh and bring the phone up to my ear. "Hi Declan," I say breathlessly.

"Are you okay?" he asks in a worried tone.

I lean against the counter and close my eyes. "Yeah, I was just unpacking a bunch of grocery bags," I lie easily.

"Oh...okay. So, ah, what's up?" he asks uncertainly. Well, damn, I really feel like shit. Damon was right. He doesn't even sound close to the sweetly obnoxious and overly confident guy that I've met.

I take a deep breath and pray that I'm not going to regret this. "I was just wondering if you were busy tonight?"

Hours later:

It's several hours after the call, in which Declan agreed, cautiously, to come over for dinner. Can't blame him for sounding wary, I'm not exactly giving him the world's best signals.

What in the hell am I doing? I ask myself as I check my reflection in the hallway mirror once again, for the third, okay twentieth time, in the past few minutes.

Declan should be here any minute now and to say that I'm freaking out would be the understatement of the year. I spent the last few hours making pierogis and a salad. I had just enough time to shower and make myself look cute. I also made sure to kick out my nosy ass roommate. Can't trust his ass after his little stunt this afternoon.

I stare at my reflection and try to see what Declan could possibly see. Sure, my eye color is pretty awesome and my hair is falling in nice shiny waves framing my face. And yeah, my lips could give Angelina Jolie a run for her money.

But I have a ton of curves and an ass that just won't quit. Okay, my brownie addiction won't quit, but still, I blame my never-ending butt.

I'm dressed in a cute tiffany blue blouse and tight dark blue jeans. You know the type of jeans that you have to lie down to get into but make everything look amazing when you're standing? Yeah, I have those babies on tonight. I also paired all this with some cute jewelry and my black booties.

All in all, I look really good and only added a minimal amount of make-up. I look cute without screaming, trying way too hard. Well, at least I hope that's how I look anyway.

Shit! I keep turning this way and that in the mirror. What if I do look like I'm trying too hard? Or he's just being nice and is coming over to telling me that he no longer wants anything to do with me and I look like I'm trying to put a move on him or something?

Maybe I should just call him back and tell him to forget all about this. Yes! That's exactly what I'll do. I'll just tell him that dinner burned or something. That's totally believable.

Just as I'm reaching for my phone, I hear a knock at my door. Son of a bitch!

I close my eyes and take a few, dozen, calming breathes to get my shit under control. I can do this. He's just a guy, a really hot and sweet guy, with abs that look painted on, but just a guy.

I open my eyes and walk calmly, I snort to myself, yeah right, to the door and pause with my hand hovering over the knob. I can do this, just open the door and let the good-looking cop in. Easy peasy girl. Just open the door and smile

"Ya know, I can tell that you're standing in front of the door," he says with humor lacing every word. "Your footsteps stopped way too close for you not to be standing on the other side."

I can feel myself turn about a million different shades of red. I quickly pull open the door and lose my breath at what I see standing on the other side.

Declan is leaning against the door jamb with his arms crossed over his muscular chest. He's wearing a white and gray checkered button-up shirt that looks like it's about to be shredded if he flexes the slightest bit. Light wash blue jeans and black boots.

His hair is styled to perfection with that little flip-up thing that only certain guys can pull off without looking douchey. Let me tell you, Declan can most definitely pull it off. He is by far the sexiest man that I've ever seen.

Annnnnd I'm just standing here like a buffoon drooling at him. "Hi," I chirp in a freakishly high voice.

His lips twitch. "Hey, Aims." I didn't realize until this moment how much I missed hearing him say that. "Can I come in, or would you like to stare at me some more first?"

And cue me turning even redder. But what can I say, I was ogling his fine self. I step aside and allow him to enter. Of course, he happens to brush up against me. I bite back a smile at his sharp intake when his forearm brushes my breasts.

Damn, if I thought the front view was amazing, the view from behind is fucking spectacular. His ass in those jeans is utterly delicious. Damn, the man really is perfection.

He looks over his shoulder and winks at me. "You gonna close the door or just keep staring at my ass?"

I narrow my eyes while pushing the door closed. "I wasn't staring," I lie terribly. "I was just trying to figure out when to serve dinner, that's all."

He turns around with a huge smile on his face. "That's seriously what you're going to go with?"

I ignore his question and point to the flowers in his hand. "For me?"

He nods almost shyly. "Yep, my mother instilled in Damon and I that we never go over to a woman's house empty-handed."

My lips twitch as I grab them from him. I bring them up to my nose and inhale. They smell divine. I look up into his eyes and smile. "Thank you. Why don't you have a seat in the living room while I put these in some water? Would you like anything to drink?"

He shakes his head no. "I'm good for now."

I nod and scurry into the kitchen, needing a small reprieve from all the raw maleness. I reach up into the cabinet and try to reach the vase on the top shelf. Freaking Brad! He doesn't seem to understand that not everyone who lives here is over six feet tall. I keep reaching and my fingers barely brush the middle.

That's when I feel the outline of a hard body pressed firmly into my back. I swallow deeply as I tilt my head back and see Declan staring down at me. He reaches above us and grabs the vase that I was unsuccessfully reaching for.

"I've got it," he says with a gravelly voice that sounds a few octaves lower than usual. He lowers the vase and places it on the counter in front of me but makes no move to leave.

With him standing so close, I can smell his spicy scent. I can't stop the deep inhale and sigh that happens entirely without my permission. Traitorous body. His strong arms cage me in from behind and my stupid body yet again does what I don't want it to and shivers at the contact.

I can feel his face against my hair. His breath tickles strands of my hair. I stand clutching the flowers close to my chest like somehow they will keep me grounded as his scent causes me to fly higher and higher.

He nuzzles the side of my head and it takes every single ounce of self-control that I possess not to purr like a damn cat. I swear he's a damn warlock or something. For as far as I can remember, my body has never reacted to anyone else like this in my life

"You better make sure that me, here, is what you really want Aimee," he says roughly. "I won't have the strength to walk away from you again. The first time gutted me. If you don't want to give whatever this is between us an honest shot, you need to tell me right now."

I close my eyes and exhale, here goes nothing. "I do want to try, but I'm scared. You're going to need to be patient when I have a freak-out or something. Because seriously, I'm crazy more days than I'm sane. I'm like nuts on the best of days. You don't even know."

I feel his body shaking and turn around to glare at him. I can tell that he's trying hard but he is not really able to keep himself from laughing. I smack his stupid washboard abs with the back of my hand. "I'm being serious and you're laughing at me."

"Hellcat, I just can't believe that you felt the need to tell me that you're crazy, like it isn't obvious."

My eyes narrow even further. "I have been like so beyond sane when I've been in your presence that it's not even funny. I've been one of the sanest women ever," I huff.

His lips twitch and he stares down at me with eyes that are swimming in mirth. "Hey Aim, have you forgotten that I've seen you drunk?"

I frown up at him. "You said that I was the best behaved that night."

"Yeah, considering whose company you were in, that's not really saying too much. But I appreciate the warning hellcat." He nuzzles my cheek again and I'm pretty sure that it's just to hide his smile.

"You know, bad things can happen to men dumb enough to laugh at a crazy woman to her face," I say casually.

He pulls back and looks down at me in amusement. "What are you going to do? Hit me with your flowers?" He snorts.

I look down and see that I'm clutching them between us and shrug. "They have thorns and those are pointy and sharp. I could do some damage with these."

I feel his body shaking even harder. "Right. Well, how about I go sit down so that you can put your chosen weapon in some water. Better safe than sorry and all that," he says with a grin before kissing my cheek and going to sit at the island.

I purse my lips. "You have no idea how dangerous I could be with these," I mutter.

"I have no doubt," he drawls.

I decide to ignore his sarcasm and finish putting the flowers into water. Once done with that, I start frying up the pierogis that I boiled earlier.

"How much butter did you just put into that pan?" he asks.

I look over my shoulder and can see that his eyes are as round as saucers. "Don't worry about that."

"Don't worry about it?" he sputters. "I can already feel my arteries clogging. Are you trying to kill me slowly?"

I roll my eyes while placing the pierogis into the sizzling butter. "I'm not trying to kill you, you big baby. You have to cook these in a lot of butter. It's usually butter and onions, but I hate onions, so just plain old butter it is."

I stir them around and flip them to make sure that they brown properly on each side. I cover them and turn towards Declan. Declan who is staring at me curiously. I raise an eyebrow. "What?"

He leans forward onto the top of the island. "You just said that you hate onions?"

I nod. "Yeah...so?" I'm sure a lot of people hate them. I don't see why he looks so weird.

"But you told me that night at the Mexican place how much you like the bloomin' onion and French onion soup."

I wave a hand in the air. "Oh, that's different."

I turn back and put the first set onto a plate before frying up some more. This is going to take a while since I made sixty of these suckers. I hope he's hungry.

"How is it different? They're all made out of onions?" he asks incredulously.

"They taste completely different. Bloomin' has that awesome sauce and the soup had bread and cheese and just perfection. It's not like just eating fried up onions on top of something. Yuck." I wrinkle my nose.

He's just sitting there staring at me. "You eat more of the onions in the soup."

I shake my head no while getting plates and silverware out. "Nope, I don't eat the onions in the soup, just the broth, bread, and cheese."

"What about the bloomin' onion then?"

"Eh, the sauce and the batter mask the taste for the most part. But once I've had enough of the onions, I just rip off the crunchy batter and dip that into the sauce."

"What in the hell is wrong with you?"

I look up and blink at him in confusion. "What are you talking about?"

His eyes widen. "What am I talking about? I'm talking about how you leave out the best and most important part of each thing that you order. Why order any of that at all then if you're not even going to eat?"

"Because I like how it tastes," I reply simply.

"How would you know; you don't actually eat it," he says.

"I do too eat it," I say in exasperation. "I just don't eat the gross parts...the onions."

"Do you have any other weird eating habits that I should know about? I feel like this is going to be incredibly important later on."

I fling my spatula around in the air. "First, I don't have weird eating habits. They're completely normal." I'm nice enough to pretend that I didn't see his eye roll. "Second, I just have certain things that I don't really eat...that's all."

Okay, I'm not going to lie, I'm a bit of a freak when it comes to eating. I know that some people think the way that I eat can be a little strange. But come on, everyone has things that they don't like. I'm just more upfront about, is all.

"And those would be?" He motions me with his hand to continue.

I turn back and start plating up the food. "Hmm, well I don't really like meat."

"You're a vegan?" he gasps with a look of disgust on his face.

I turn and look at him like he's dumb because well he is. "I ordered a BLT at lunch. I'm obviously not a vegan. I just don't like steak, or hamburgers, or pork chops, or well most types of meat really. Well except for kielbasa and kabanosy, but that's just a polish thing."

"What are those?" he asks warily. Good grief this guy.

"Polish version of smoked sausage basically. Kabanosy is amazing with horseradish on it. I can seriously eat an entire ring all by myself it's so good."

He nods his head without blinking. "Okay, what else?"

I bring the plates to the island and sit beside him. I hand him his silverware and grab my own. I start to cut into my food before answering. "I won't eat meat at any restaurants. The only time that I'll eat chicken and ground beef is if I prepare it myself. I won't even eat it if my mother cooks it. I just can't seem to do it for some reason."

"So, let me see if I have this correct," he says before pausing and eating a pierogi whole. Men are so gross some days. I won't lie though, his moan of appreciation does some funny things to my core. "These are really good," he says through his mouthful of food.

I give him a smirk. "I'm glad you like them. They took forever to make."

"Worth it." He shoves another one into his mouth. "So, what do you eat when you go out?"

I hand him a napkin and shake my head at the vulture that he seems to have become. "Pasta or seafood mainly." I shrug while taking small, normal human-sized bites of my food. He's right though, these came out perfect.

He gives me a look that I can't place. "Well, at least you didn't say salad. Pasta and seafood I can work with," he says like it really matters that he's okay with what I choose to eat.

I can't even help my reply. "My life's goal is now complete," I drawl.

It's been a few weeks since Aimee decided to give me an actual chance. I'm not really sure what changed her mind but I'm happy as hell. Getting to spend time with her has been incredible so far. I enjoy the fact that she can give Kayla a run for her money when it comes to being salty.

I probably shouldn't enjoy our verbal sparring sessions as much as I do. But I love a woman with a ton of wit and sass. I never have to worry about being bored whenever we're together. Which unfortunately is not as much as I would really like.

Between her work schedule and mine, we are only able to really see each other three, maybe four times a week tops. Who knew that her having to work every other weekend would be such a pain in the ass? Not that I don't have to as well...but still.

And since she had to work this weekend, Damon and I made plans to meet up to get in some range time. I'll get to spend the day with my brother and then go and bring dinner to my woman. Perfect day if you ask me.

"Must you smile so much?" my extremely loving twin asks.

I look over at where he's sitting while putting his rifle together and smile even wider. "If it annoys you, absolutely."

"I liked you better when you were moping around."

"I love when you whisper sweet nothings to me," I reply dryly.

He rolls his eyes at me while finishing up. "I'm happily married and you don't see me smiling nonstop."

I'm sitting a little way down on the bench from him. I'm only shooting my service gun today and don't have as much work as he has. He likes to keep his skills sharp behind the scope, so we'll most likely spend a decent amount of time doing that. Ah, just like the good old days, getting to spot.

My lips twitch. "I'm pretty sure the world would end if you cracked a smile."

He stares at me for a moment before looking down again. "I smile," he mutters.

"I know you do," I reply in honesty. It's true, he does smile, but only around a certain few. Me, Michelle, Jax, mom, and dad are the only ones that he'll smile for. And maybe Mellie, but I think he's usually laughing at something that she tripped over mostly.

"Right. Anyway, Aimee good?" he asks.

I blink a few times because he's never actually asked about any of the women that I've dated in the past. Not that there have been any recently, but past ones were never asked about. "Ah, yeah?"

He frowns at me. "You don't know if your woman is good?" He tilts his head in confusion.

I shake my head slowly. "No, I know she's good. I'm just confused as to why you're asking about her."

"She's important to you, why wouldn't I ask?" he counters while creepily stroking his rifle. I wonder if he even realizes that he's doing it.

"You never asked about anyone else I've dated." I shrug.

He nods his head slowly like I'm an idiot. "Like I said, she's important to you."

"She's doing good," is all I can say because I'm a bit stunned. Not that he picked up on the fact that she's important to me. But the fact that he's right, none of the others ever were. Huh, that kind of makes me sound like an asshole. I shrug internally...oh well.

"You two get shit straightened out?" he grunts out before going to stand in one of the lanes.

I nod my head. "Yeah, we did." I tilt my head and really look at my brother. "You know something has been bothering for a few weeks now."

He looks over his shoulder at me. "I'm sure a prescription of penicillin will clear that right up."

I sigh. "I wish other people knew how bad your jokes were and how much I suffer having to deal with them."

"You know that was funny," he replies without turning around. It was, but I'll never admit it.

"No, what's been bothering me is the fact that she just called me up out of the blue to come over for dinner. It just doesn't make any sense since she was so against actually giving me a shot."

You see, I've had a few suspicions as to why she just randomly gave me a call. Did she regret pushing me away? Probably, but she's stubborn, she wouldn't give in to herself that easily. No, I think that someone else might've given her a helpful *"push."* And I'm pretty sure that we shared a womb.

"Maybe she's just smart enough to realize what a stupendous catch you are," he drawls.

"Look at you using big words. And you know damn well what I'm asking. To quote you, *"you ain't dumb."*

He turns around to face me and leans against the lane with his arms crossed over his chest. We have a good old- fashioned stare down like we used to have when we were kids. Who says that you actually have to grow up when you become an adult?

70

It probably lasts a lot longer than it should, but losing to the other is a worse fate than death. We both have tears streaming down our faces before we both give the tie signal. We had to come up with it when we were younger for moments just like this.

After taking a few moments each to blink repeatedly, we look at each other with a smirk.

"I might've bumped into her when I was out grocery shopping a few weeks ago," he admits.

"You don't say?" I drawl.

He shrugs unapologetically. "You were unhappy. I decided to do something about it."

I narrow my eyes and cross my arms. "Did you threaten her to be with me?" I don't really think that he would...but.

"Never mind, I was wrong, you are dumb."

I roll my eyes. "I had to make sure. With you, it's better to be safe than sorry. So, no threatening was involved. I'm proud of you," I say as condescendingly as humanly possible.

He gives me an odd frown. "She's not intimidated by me."

I push my legs out in front of me and cross my ankles. "How do you know?"

"She told me," he replies simply. Yeah, that's not going to fly.

"Why would she feel the need to tell you that Dam?" My eyes widen. "You did try to scare her into being with me? What the actual fuck?" I shriek.

"I didn't try to scare her. I just wasn't overly nice at first...or at all."

"What else?"

"Nothing. She told me that I don't scare her and I told her that you like to eat. That's all."

I give him a dubious look because come on...it's him. "That was your entire conversation?" I doubt that. I doubt it very much.

"Yup," he says with his stubborn look on. The look that means he won't be saying anything else.

"Fine." I sigh. "But can you try to be nice from now on?" I hold up my hand when he goes to reply. "I know, your kind of nice. I don't need you to be her best friend, but I would prefer you not to be your usual asshole self."

He shrugs his massive shoulders. "No skin off my ass."

"You're so eloquent some days. You make mom so proud."

He ignores me and turns around to fire his weapon. He looks back at me with an annoyed look. "You going to get off your ass so we can do this? Or you gonna sit there thinking about how mom loves me more?"

I snort but get up and walk over to him. "Don't act like you don't know that I'm mom's favorite."

He side-eyes me for a minute. "How do you figure?"

I give him a winning smile. "Because you set more fires when learning to cook than I did. She really loved those ugly, puke green dish towels."

His lips twitch. "Yeah, it was a real shame that those seemed to go up in flames first."

We both smile at each other before getting down to business for the rest of the day.

Hours Later:

After spending the rest of the day shooting with Damon, I had just enough time to get some pizza and get to Aimee's place. I would much rather be all alone at my place, but I get that she's tired and wants to be in her own space after a long day at work. Plus, she has to get up crazy early to be back at the hospital for seven the next morning anyway.

We've yet to take that final step, shall we say. Not that it doesn't seem like we both want to. It just seems like there is an invisible force keeping us from going further. Either her roommate comes home and kills the mood.

Or like a few days, just as I was about to get a condom, I ended up getting called in for a SWAT call. It's like we can't catch a *fucking* break. Yeah, you know that pun was intended.

I'm pretty sure that my dick is going to revolt if it doesn't get inside of her soon. He's already popping up to say hi at inconvenient times just to let me know that he's still there and he still wants her.

It's like I'm a teenager unable to control my boner again. I swear, all she has to do is walk into the room and smile at me and I'm fucking hard. You don't even want to know how much time my hand and dick have been spending together. I think I'm even getting calluses again just like my teenage self had.

And isn't that some shit? I'm a grown-ass man, with a gorgeous and very willing woman and I'm still stuck using my hand! We need to catch a break soon before I kidnap her for real this time and take her away to a place with no cell service. Trust me, that only sounds creepy, it really isn't...at all.

I knock on her door and hear shuffling inside. The lock turns and I'm greeted with the sight of Brad, in a towel and nothing else. I'm secure enough to admit that if he was straight, I'd be worried about him and Aimee living together.

He motions me inside and closes the door behind me. I walk over to the kitchen counter and drop the pizza box on top. I turn around and ask him something that's been bugging me for a while.

"How did Stacey not realize you were gay?" I never said that I was the most tactful man in the world.

He blinks at me a few times before smiling. "You're wondering if we ever had sex you mean?" He hits the nail on the head.

I nod. "It's kind of a big part of a relationship."

He fixes his towel and sits on one of the island stools. "It is, but she had met my parents and knew how religious and sanctimonious they are. I was terrified of coming out, so I told her that I wanted to wait until marriage."

My eyebrows raise to my hairline. "And she just went along with that?"

He smiles genuinely. "Yes and no. You've met?" I nod. "She's one of the sweetest women in the world. So, yeah, she would go along with something like that. But she had also gotten out of a really rough relationship before we met. I think that she liked the stability of having me in her life. We truly were just best friends who said that they were dating. I think she always suspected but just went along with it anyway."

I tilt my head. "Yeah, I guess that makes sense."

He places his arms on the island and steeples them together. "Plus, I'm not overly outrageous like most gay men are stereotyped. I'm still me and like to watch sports, I just happen to like a side of beef."

I give him a drool look. "You just had to go there huh?"

He gives me a wide smile and a shrug. "Couldn't help myself." He starts to get up and catches his towel before it falls. "Well, I'm going to go dressed so that you two love birds can have some privacy for once." He wiggles his eyebrows causing me to laugh.

"You don't have to leave your own place man," I say to be polite as I'm mentally calculating how long until he leaves.

He snorts like he can read my thoughts. "Right. Well, as nice as it is of you to say that, you're not the only one with a hot date tonight."

"That dating app is working out for you?"

He starts walking down the hall. "So far so good!"

I decide to make myself useful and plate up a few slices. I also pour a glass of wine for Aimee since the last time we spoke today she asked me if I would be willing to hide a few bodies for her. I took that to mean that she wasn't having an overly pleasant day.

I pour the normal amount of wine into a glass and then mentally say fuck it and pour it to the rim. I'm sure that she'll appreciate not needing to get a refill too soon. I pop the top on my beer and take a sip, reveling in the cold liquid going down my throat.

I hear a noise from the mouth of the hallway and look over to see her staring at me.

I give her a smirk. "See something you like?"

She nods her head seriously. "Yup, pizza and wine."

She walks over to the wine and takes a big sip and sighs.

My lips twitch. "You know, if I was any less secure, I would be hurt that you skipped right over me."

She smiles widely at me. "Today has been one of those days that you shouldn't even try to compete with the wine. Because I guarantee you, that you will lose. Wine is life tonight and the pizza is my cuddle buddy."

I slide the plate of pizza that she's drooling over towards her. "This conversation is so wrong, on so many different levels."

She takes a gigantic bite of her pizza, making me proud. Her moan of appreciation goes straight to my dick. Dammit, I was doing really well so far tonight.

"Babe?"

"What?" she says around her mouthful. We keep it so classy some days.

"You need to stop making noises like that while Brad's still here," I tell her seriously. She makes some more noises like that and I'm likely to fuck her on top of the island regardless of whether or not he can walk in.

She blinks a few times while chewing. "You can't compete with the pizza right now either." Such a shit.

Brad barks out a laugh as he enters the room again, this time fully dressed.

Aimee gives him a once over and raises an eyebrow. "Someone is trying to get lucky tonight," she states.

I look at him and then back at her in confusion. "How can you tell? He's wearing jeans and a button-down shirt. None of that screams, 'I'm on the prowl.' He looks pretty covered up."

He smirks while she just downright laughs at me. "Brad, flex and cross your arms." He does and his white shirt looks like it's about to rip. "This is his, 'I'm trying to get some, without looking like I'm trying to get some' shirt. It's white and tight and he, of course, rolls the sleeves up to his forearms. He may as well just wear some grey sweatpants and a white muscle shirt out. He would look like less of a slut."

They're both cackling like a couple of hens, making me even more confused. I can feel my brow furrow. "Okay, I was with you until the sweat pants thing."

They both look at each other with eyes full of mischief. Brad seems to take pity on me first. "Grey sweat pants dude, how have you not heard about that? Women talk about it all the time."

I roll my eyes. "You're a gay man. Of course, they talk to you about shit like that. Straight men aren't usually involved in conversations about other men. We tend to frown on that," I drawl.

He purses his lips in thought. "Okay, yeah, that makes sense. I'll try to explain it to you then, in a straight way that you'll understand." I just motion for him to hurry up. "You ever want to get laid at any time, no matter what, wear grey sweatpants and nothing else."

Aimee slaps him on the chest with one hand while shoving a slice of pizza into her mouth with the other. I like that she can multi-task like that.

I raise my eyebrows in question. "You're serious?" And he nods his head. "Why the hell would that work. I mean, I can see my abs doing the trick." I ignore the fact that they both roll their eyes at me. "But I don't get why the color of my sweatpants matters."

He looks evilly at me for a moment. "Are you sure that you want to know? You'll never be able to unknow this."

"Yeah, I'm sure." For real, what's the big deal?

"Dick print," he states casually before swooping in and taking a bite out of Aimee's pizza. That's a brave man. I've seen the way she looks at food.

My beer bottle is frozen midway to my mouth. "I'm going to regret this but what the hell does that mean?" I ask and then take a huge gulp of beer. I have a feeling that alcohol is going to be required for the rest of this conversation.

Brad is standing far away from Aimee who's glaring at him. I'm just not sure if it's over the conversation choice or the pizza. Who am I kidding? It's the pizza.

"Okay, but don't say that I didn't warn you. Dick print is what happens when a guy wears grey sweat pants. Especially if he's sans boxers, you get the full effect and outline. It's basically the guy equivalent of wearing a mini skirt without panties. Women go crazy for it. They have a ton of memes online and stuff about it. Most women in relationships will never let their man out of the house in grey sweatpants."

There is so much to process right now. I look over at Aimee who has just finished, I shit you not, her fourth slice of pizza and is delicately wiping her mouth. She really is the woman for me.

I raise an eyebrow at my woman. "You would say something if I left the house in grey sweatpants?"

She snorts into her wine and starts laughing. "It's funny that you think that I would ever let you leave the house looking like a whore." She reaches up and pats my cheek. "You're so cute some days."

Brad does a *Vanna White* impersonation with his hands. "And there you have it," he says smugly.

"This night is a lot weirder than I thought it would be," I say to no one in particular.

Brad chuckles. "Welcome to life with Aimee."

He deftly moves out of the half-assed punch she throws in his direction. I think the fact that she's holding her wine was a big factor of her sad attempt. But I have seen her choke while eating...so maybe not.

"Alright love birds, I'm off to hopefully meet the man of my dreams. Wish me luck."

"Don't put out on the first date!" Aimee says at the same time I say, "Look out for cold sores." We look at each other and smile.

Brad look between the two of us with pursed lips. "I don't know if I should be happy that she found someone as much as an asshole as she is, or if I should be worried."

"Don't you have a bad decision to go and try to pick up?" I drawl.

"And to think that I actually rooted for you." He sniffs before giving us both the finger and walking out the door.

"He's such a big baby some days." Aimee chuckles while throwing out her paper plate. I notice that Aimee hates cleaning so much that they have the cabinets stocked with paper plates. I have to say, it is convenient though.

I start shoveling food into my mouth to try to catch up. She was like a freaky, pizza-eating ninja or some shit. I didn't even really see her inhale a few of them. I only know how many she ate because of how many are missing from the damn box. It's honestly really impressive and a tad bit frightening.

"Do you think that I was too hard on him?" I don't want to offend him. I just don't usually filter too much of what comes out of my mouth.

Aimee snorts and then her eyes widen. "Oh, you're serious?" I nod my head while taking another bite of pizza as she lapses into an explanation. "His parents literally called him every horrible slur that you can think of and then disowned him. You joking with him, is not going to hurt his feelings. Trust me, he likes that you treat him like everyone else."

The revelation leaves me shaking with anger that I have to push down before speaking. "I can't believe that his parents actually did that. I couldn't imagine having a son and just abandoning him because of his sexual orientation. It just seems stupid to me. It's your kid no matter who they love."

She blinks at me a few times and I purposely ignore what looks like tears. I do not handle those things well at all. I still have a minor freak out whenever I do something nice for my mom and she starts crying her "happy tears" as she calls them. Tears are damn tears; I don't do any of them.

"You really mean that, don't you?" she says.

I pause mid-bite and look at her in confusion. "Yeah, why wouldn't I?" I finish taking my bite and chew while she answers.

She gives me an adorably sheepish shrug. "I dunno. Most guys don't say too much about him being gay. But they aren't overly horrified by what his parents did either."

"That's because Dam and I grew up with it being normal. Our dad's best friend since childhood is gay. He and his partner have been together for about thirty years now. We didn't even realize that there was so much prejudice against gay people until we were older and heard things that people would say. To us, it just never made a difference. Cal and Dan are still our pseudo-uncles no matter what."

"Too bad not everyone is raised like that," she grumbles into her wine.

"I agree. Mom and dad gave us something very special by having Cal and Dan in our lives. We were raised without the hate and fear a lot of people are raised with. I'll always be grateful my parents are so loving."

She sighs loudly. "Too bad that your parents couldn't have been his as well. I swear that I've never seen anyone as hurt and dejected as he was after what his parents said. It took everything that I had to not go after them. I literally had to hold Stacey back, when all I really wanted to do was let her go."

He gives me a funny-looking smirk before shaking his head. "I can't really picture Stacey being mad enough to go after someone. She is honestly the most mild-tempered woman that I've ever met."

I nod my head because he is correct for the most part because she normally is. "You're right, except when it comes to people that she cares about. Then she becomes an angry Pitbull who is ready to tear you to shreds." I take a rather large sip of my wine before asking him the question that's been on my mind since he walked through the door. "So, what would you like to do tonight?"

"You," he says the words so casually that I'm taken by surprise and begin to choke on my wine.

He walks over and starts patting my back. "I'm really beginning to become concerned over the fact that you choke so easily. I feel like you shouldn't be left unsupervised when you're eating or drinking."

I regain control and glare up at the jerk who is barely holding back his smile. I swat his hand away. "I was fine until you came into my life. I'm really beginning to think that you're a jinx."

His eyes narrow at me and he places his hands on his tapered waist. "Take that back."

I give him a smirk and shake my head slowly. "Nope," I tell him while popping the p just to be annoying.

His eyes have suddenly gone from dark brown to black. "You sure that you don't want to change your answer hellcat? Bad things can happen to stubborn women with smart mouths," he says calmly but the excitement in his eyes betray him.

I walk up to him slowly and calmly, even though my insides are quivering, but not with fear. The look in his eyes is primal and it's the most exciting and sexiest thing that I've ever seen. When I'm in front of him, I run my hands up and down his chest and stomach. He wasn't lying earlier; his abs really could make a woman do almost anything. He makes a hissing sound when I use my nails on the way down. I look up at him with wide, innocent-looking eyes.

"And what's going to happen if I don't take it back?" I whisper. "We both know that you would never hurt me." Well, physically anyway, but I keep that part to myself.

He places his hands on my hips and grips the sides tightly, but not painfully so. He lowers his head and nuzzles against the side of my neck. I can feel his hot breath wash over me. "Are you sure that you want to find out? There's no going back after this. You'll be mine and only mine."

I snort without meaning to. He gives me a curious look that I just smile at. "Declan, I've been all yours since you asked me if I was going to frisk you."

I'm not really sure what happens next. It's almost like some invisible line snaps. Declan goes from still to in motion in under a second. I'm up in his arms, my legs wrapped around his waist, his hands on my ass, and he's walking towards my bedroom before I even realize what's going on.

Not that there's a chance in hell that I'll complain. I have been dying to get this man in my bed and be uninterrupted for a long time now. The apocalypse could be upon us and I would tell him to keep going. This is happening tonight come hell or high water.

We're in my bedroom in what seems like the blink of an eye. Kicking the door shut, he places me gently on the bed and I stare at him. Even in the dark, I can see his face. Its burned into my memory.

I'm not really sure what had gotten into me out there. I'm not usually so brazen. Actually, yes, I do. His response when I asked him what he wanted to do tonight inflamed me like no one else ever has before.

But now that we're in here and this is actually going to happen, I've now come down with a case of the nerves. I know that I shouldn't but the man standing above me is pure perfection. And let's face it, I'm totally not. The last time that we even got close to having sex, I managed to somehow keep my shirt on.

I have a feeling that I won't be that lucky tonight with the way that he's staring at me.

Seriously, how the hell am I supposed to get naked in front of a man who looks like he was carved out of freaking stone? I'm not fat per se, but you can definitely tell that I don't say no to cookies, or brownies, or tacos, or wine or beer...well you get the point. My damn rolls have rolls and here's this gorgeous creature standing above me.

Maybe I should fake a headache? Oh, I know! I could tell him that I'm cold and need to keep my shirt on. My legs are in decent shape thanks to being on them so much. I begin to think that I can make this work!

He's looking down at me with his head tilted. "What are you thinking about?"

I blink up at him a few times. "Why?"

"Because you had a ton of emotions cross your face. Some were apprehensive and then the last one was a weird triumphant one. Honestly, you're kind of making me nervous."

I bite my lip. "I was just thinking that I'm cold."

"You're cold?" He purses his lips.

"Ah, yeah. I should probably keep my shirt on to keep warm."

The smile that he gives me is downright feral. "Don't worry, I'll make sure that you stay heated up all night."

He's not falling for it. I scramble for another excuse. "Ahh, well I'm sure that you will. But I would still prefer to keep my shirt on and get under the covers."

He was climbing up onto the bed but pauses mid crawl. "Aims, is there a reason that you don't want to take your clothes off? Because I've got to tell you, hellcat, it's eighty degrees outside, so I'm not really buying the whole cold thing."

Well shit. I kind of forgot that we're having an unusually warm spring. I wonder if I could convince him that I'm anemic and cold no matter what the temperature?

I look up into his skeptical eyes and decide that he probably won't be buying that anytime soon. Dammit. I bite my lower lip and then blow out a big breath. Screw it. "I don't want you to see me naked," I rush out.

He nods slowly. "Yeah, I've picked up on that part baby. I'm just trying to figure out why not."

I snort without meaning to. "Are you kidding me right now? How the hell can you have no idea?"

He gives me a careless shrug. "Probably because I don't have hormones that turn me into a psycho?"

My eyes turn to slits. "That answer isn't really something that you should say if you're planning on getting laid," I growl.

"Eh, I figure that I can just whip off my shirt and show you my abs."

I snap my fingers. "And that's why I don't want to get totally naked!"

He gives me an adorably confused look. "Because you like my abs?"

I look up at the ceiling and pray for strength. "Not because I like your abs, you big dope. Because I don't want to get naked next to someone who has like one percent body fat when I have like ninety percent. You have to know that I'm not tiny like other women."

He shuffles himself in front of me so that we're eye to eye. "Yes, I'm very aware of what your body looks like."

"Then you have to get that I don't want all my fat out and on display."

"Hellcat, you are not even close to fat," he says with an annoying smirk.

"Well, I'm definitely not thin. I have tummy rolls and my ass could double as a shelf," I pout with my arms crossed.

Damn, how did we go from sexy time to this? Oh yeah, that's right...I'm a neurotic freak. Just kill me now.

He bursts out laughing. It actually takes him a moment to get himself under control. "Aims, trust me, no man wants to fuck a skeleton." I sputter but he ignores me. "And second, trust me, that ass of yours should be worshiped regularly. It is a thing of beauty. You have no idea how many assholes I've watched almost break their necks trying to catch another glimpse. It takes a lot of effort not to throat punch some of them."

"Seriously?" I ask him incredulously.

He nods sagely. "Yeah, we might have to think about getting you some baggy pants or something. Even your fucking scrub pants mold to your ass." He groans.

"Yeah, that won't be happening." I am not trying to make myself look any bigger. Every woman knows that wearing baggy clothes does not help you out at all.

He narrows his eyes and looks to his left. "We'll see," he mutters before turning back to me with a bright smile. "Plus, I've already seen you naked."

My eyes go huge. "When?"

He gives me a wicked smirk. "The night that you and all the girls thought that you could drink your weight in margaritas. You decided to change in front of me. I actually tried to leave the room but you whined because you wanted me to stay and cuddle." He chuckles.

"Why didn't you ever tell me that?" I shriek.

He rubs the back of his neck and gives me a sheepish look. "I figured that you would then realize what I've been jerking off to."

I blink and shake my head trying to get my brain working again. I'm not going to lie. It short-circuited at the thought of him stroking himself. "Kayla is right, there is something really wrong with you."

He narrows his eyes and then pounces on me. I'm flat on my back with him above me before I even know what's happening. He brings his face down to mine. "You need to stop listening to MSG. Her salty ass is bad for you. Just look at who she's married to."

I raise my eyebrow. "You mean I shouldn't be friends with two of your best friends?" I drawl.

"I'm fully okay if you hate those two and never want to go near them, ever again. I'll support your decision," he says sadly.

"And if I want to spend every weekend with them?"

"I don't support that...at all."

I start laughing at the crazy man on top of me. "You're absolutely ridiculous, do you know that?"

He grabs my face in his hands and gives me an imploring look. "I'm serious, that whole family is bad for you. Those angelic-looking children were ready to shank Marc. You don't want to be anywhere near all that crazy."

I give him a sideways glance because Kayla has told me about this. "Didn't Marc keep bitching about how the kids were putting the dishes into the dishwasher and making them take them out and redo it all over again if they got it wrong?"

"Yeah...so?"

I scoff. "So? I'd want to stab his annoying ass too if I was them."

He shakes his head sadly. "I don't understand how crazy people keep ending up in my life."

I give him a drool look. "Ever think that it might just be you? That we were all fine before we met you?"

"Obviously not since I'm amazing," he says in total seriousness. This man has absolutely no self-esteem issues, that's for damn sure.

"Right."

His eyes turn into half slits and he wrinkles his nose. "You don't agree? And I want you to think long and hard," yes, this dope made sure to grind himself against me when he said that, "before you answer. You're in a very precarious position right now."

I raise my eyebrow. We both know that he would never hurt me. He's as cuddly as a puppy towards me. I just give him a smirk. "Is that so?" He nods his head. "And what are you going to do? Bore me to death with tales of how awesome you are?"

He gives me a nasty look that I can't help but giggle at. "First, I am awesome and you're lucky to hear about it." He growls exactly like his twin. "And second, let's not forget that you're extremely ticklish hellcat. It would be such a shame if I sat on you and tickled you until you swore that I am the most awesome man that has ever lived."

I scoff. "Good Lord, your ego is ridiculous. Seriously, you need to go to like a twelve-step program for people with delusions of grandeur."

"It's not a delusion if it's true. I'm giving you three seconds hellcat."

I try to push his heavy ass body off of me to no avail. "You can't be serious," I scoff.

He just nods his head while pinning me in place. "One."

I narrow my eyes. "Knock it off Declan."

"Two."

"I mean it. You will never get anywhere near me again," I lie horribly.

"Three," he sighs out while shaking his head sadly. "I tried to help you out."

"Declan," I growl.

In a flash, he has my arms pinned above my head and held with one hand. The other is tickling my sides like an asshole. I'm completely unable to move and just screech and laugh uncontrollably.

"Who's the most awesome, amazing and best-looking man that you've ever met?" the man that I'll soon be dumping asks.

I refuse to let him win. Over my dead body. "Damon," I reply.

He stills and looks down at me in shock. "I can not believe that you just said that."

While he's distracted, I wiggle my way out from under him. I shrug innocently. "What? Don't forget that you're the Loki and not the Thor."

He clutches his chest. "I can't believe it. I've been betrayed by my own woman. A woman who is going to get it now."

I try to get away but he pounces too fast. I'm surprised by his agility. Shouldn't someone his size move with the same speed as a sloth? I'm on my stomach trying to crawl away while laughing. Somehow, he manages to get my shirt, bra, and yoga pants off in record time. I definitely don't plan on asking him how he got so good at that. I'm a nurse, I'm supposed to help save lives, not kill the bitches who came before me.

He's back to tickling me and I'm flopping around like a fish on dry land while trying unsuccessfully to get away from him. How I end up on my back again with him between my legs, I'll never know. He's some weird *Jedi* body master. I can't help my snort. God, I'm even a geek during sexy times.

"Are you laughing at me?" he asks curiously while pinning my damn arms yet again. I swear, if I wasn't so interested in a certain body part, I would have tried to knee him already.

I shake my head. "No, I'm laughing at myself for being such a nerd."

He slowly looks my body up and down. His eyes getting darker and darker by the second. "Trust me Aims, there is absolutely nothing nerdy about you," he states roughly.

And cue my entire body turning fire engine red. I don't even reply because it's just hit me that I'm naked except for a pair of barely-there bright pink lace panties. How the hell I didn't realize it sooner, I have no idea.

I start trying in earnest to cover myself, which is obviously pointless. My arms are in his hand and his whole body is between my legs. I'm completely at his mercy. Though, I didn't expect to feel this electrified. I thought that I would feel nervous and embarrassed.

I see the raw appreciation shining from his dark orbs, I am far from embarrassed. Maybe a little nervous but I have a feeling that's just pure excitement.

He's looking down at me and smirks when he gets to my panties. He gives me a curious look. "Neon pink huh? Did you think that I wouldn't be able to find the promised land?"

I roll my eyes. Leave it to Declan to still make me smile when I want nothing more than to ravish his ridiculously perfect body. "They're not neon, they're just really pink," I mutter. "And they're pretty."

He nods his head very seriously. "I agree. They're very pretty and attached to what I'm sure is the prettiest pussy that I've ever seen." I just make a weird croaking sound at his dirty words. This man is truly lethal. "Unfortunately, no matter how pretty these panties are on you, I have no doubt that they'll look even prettier on your bedroom floor."

I feel a sharp tug and hear the unmistakable sound of my panties ripping. I look down and see that I am no longer wearing them. Declan is holding the tattered piece of fabric in his hand. "Did you just rip off my underwear?" I gasp. "Those were one of my favorite pairs!"

He gives me a wicked smirk and tosses them over his right shoulder. "Don't worry hellcat, I'll buy you a dozen more pairs that I can rip off of you."

Holy shit is my last coherent thought before his lips are on mine again in a bruising kiss that lets me know that he plans on owning me. Not that I'll object. Quite the opposite really.

I'm not sure how long the kiss lasts. It feels like a lifetime and a second all the same. It was definitely long enough to cause my core to quiver with excitement. The peach fuzz hairs along my body are standing up due to the electrifying kiss.

A harsh gasp bursts from my throat when Declan grabs ahold of my butt and grinds himself into my core. He drags one of my legs over his hip as he slides his soft, wet tongue past my teeth.

Moaning softly, I touch my tongue to his before they begin dueling for dominance. Our kiss deepens as I grip the back of his neck. However, I'm unsure if it's to ground myself or to make sure that he can't get away from me.

Rolling my hips causes Declan to groan and it's the sexiest sound that I've ever heard. I bunch the material of his t-shirt before trying to pull it off of him. I want this man naked...like yesterday.

In a swift move that only men seem to be able to pull off, Dec removes his shirt, barely breaking our kiss to do so. Feeling his heated skin against my own, makes my eyes want to roll into the back of my head. His light dusting of chest hair is rubbing against my aching breasts in the most delicious of ways.

Declan splays the hand that is not currently holding himself up against my ribcage. The space between his thumb and index finger are cradling my breast. I arch my back in a silent plea that my observant man doesn't miss. He tears his mouth from mine, our breaths harsh and ragged are mingling in the small space that he's now created.

Declan's gaze meets mine and the dark, primal, and swirling desire that I find there makes my skin ripple. This man has the face of an angel and the mouth of a devil. I am so screwed! Well...not yet, but soon.

"Pants...off," I manage to gasp out incoherently. Luckily, Declan is a smart man.

"Your wish is my favorite command." He grins salaciously.

His pants and boxers are off in record time. Damn, the man really does have some skills. He even magically produced a condom from seemingly thin air. I wonder if the military made him this efficient? I mentally slap myself. Why the hell am I even thinking about that shit right now?

Dammit! I missed watching him roll the condom down his more than colossal length. Lord, I mean he's tall but he isn't that tall. I guess he does have a right to think so highly of himself. I really hope that it fits, because it's not looking like it will, that's for damn sure.

"What's wrong?" Declan asks me seriously. "Do you want to stop? It might kill me but I will."

I nod and then shake my head. "Um, I'm just a little worried," I say sheepishly.

He blinks at me. "About what? I haven't been with anyone in years, so I'm clean. And we have a condom to prevent pregnancy."

Men! I swear to God. "I didn't mean it like that."

"Ah, okay?" he says uncertainly.

I bite my lower lip while staring at the behemoth between his legs. "It's just been a really long time for me."

"I'm extremely grateful for that."

I give him a drool look. "Really?"

He shrugs and gives me a boyish grin. "What? Don't act like you aren't happy that I haven't been with anyone in years too."

I nod. "Well, yeah...wait...what?"

"I've already told you that I haven't dated anyone because of the bet."

I look at him with wide eyes. "Yeah, but I kind of figured that you...ya know...just kept it quiet."

He gives me a blank stare. "Have you met the nosey asses that I consider my family?"

"Okay yeah, that makes sense. But as I was saying," I give him a look daring him to interrupt. "It's been a long time, which means that I'm going to be super tight."

"Are you trying to get me to blow my load before I get inside of you?"

"Declan!" I hiss. "Focus!"

He starts rubbing his hands up and down my sides, just barely brushing the underside of my breasts. "Oh, I am hellcat, I am," he says gravely.

"I'm just trying to tell you to go slow, you sex-crazed dope!" I huff while wiggling myself down a bit so that his hands stop teasing me and get to the good parts.

"Telling your man that you're really tight is not the way to get him to go slow Aims. That's a sure-fire way to get him to slam into home."

I look up at the ceiling and ask for divine guidance or maybe something to slap him with. "Holy shit, will you just get inside of me already? I am so sorry that I said anything!"

He nods his head. "You and me both."

"For the love of..." The rest of my sentence is cut off by Declan slamming his lips to mine. Thank God!

I can tell this kiss is different from the others. This one is slower and more sensual. He caresses every inch of my mouth with his tongue while running his hands all over my body. Well, everywhere except where I want him the most. I keep rolling my hips to try to get some friction.

He finally kneads one of my breasts, causing a deep moan to be pulled from my throat. He takes my nipple in-between his fingers and rolls the sensitive bud between them. He adds a little bit of pressure. Nothing painful, but enough of a pinch to ramp up my arousal to soaring heights.

I pull my lips away from him. "Please, Dec, I need you," I plead shamelessly.

He gives me a smirk and nudges his cock against my opening. He starts to slowly enter me, causing us both to moan in appreciation. The girth of him stretches me, causing a slight burning sensation that only intensifies my arousal.

Dec buries himself to the hilt, our hips pressing together firmly before he starts to slowly withdraw. A shiver slides down my spine as I tighten my legs around his hips. The hand that is not holding him up grabs my ass in a grip that I'm pretty certain is going to leave a handprint.

"Damn, hellcat. You're so fucking tight..." he growls out into my ear. He brings his face down so that our foreheads are touching. The move so sweet and intimate, that it's almost too much...almost.

His pace is slow, almost teasingly so, but I just hold on, savoring every minute of feeling him inside of me.

Our lips meet again and our tongues wrap around each other much like our bodies have. He's beginning to pick up the pace of his thrusts. They are becoming faster and harder, the more that he's losing control.

"O-o-o-o-o-oh my God Dec, harder, please," I beg as I tilt my hips to match his rhythm.

I look up into his eyes and see that they look pure black. And then suddenly I'm face down on my pillow. Dec pulls my ass up into the air and I look over my shoulder with an eyebrow raised in question.

He's kneeling behind me and is still continuing to pound into me. He didn't even break our contact when he unceremoniously flipped me over. Yeah...I won't be asking where he learned that move.

He gives me a shrug without slowing himself down. The sight of his hands gripping my hips while he thrust into me from behind is definitely going to be replaying on my mental reel for years to come. "You said that you wanted it harder."

"You still could've given me some warning," I pant like a damn dog. Way to be sexy Aims.

He gives me a wink and a slap to my right butt cheek. "Where's the fun in that?"

I shake my head and turn my head to face forward again. I grip the sheets so tightly that my knuckles are turning white. But God help me, the man is doing as he was told. My entire body is bouncing with the force of his thrusts.

I eventually have to place my hands on the headboard to make sure that my face doesn't smack into it.

My breaths are coming out in short pants and I can feel the sweat dripping down my spine as I try to meet him thrust for thrust. The only sound that I can hear is our breathing and the slapping of our skin.

"You need to cum soon baby, I don't think that I can hold out much longer," he says in a hoarse voice.

I whimper. "I need...I need."

"I got you, hellcat," he says as he moves one hand to my mound. His fingers find my clit and he begins to rub furious circles causing me to gasp.

"Oh God," I moan.

"It's Declan, but you can call me God. I'm generous like that." I just roll my eyes at the bonehead whose ego is definitely bigger than his head.

I can feel an earth-shattering and mind-rendering orgasm begin to take hold. My feet are arching and I can feel my inner muscles begin to clamp down.

"Shit," Declan hisses out. His thrusts are becoming jerky and less graceful. His hands are gripping my sides hard enough to leave imprints. "Your pussy is gripping my dick like it's trying to milk me for everything that I've got. Cum for me now hellcat."

It's as if he has total control over my body. The orgasm washes over me like a tidal wave at his works. I suck in a gulp of air through my teeth and hold it as I ride this blissful wave for as long as humanly possible.

I can feel Declan still behind me, while groaning loudly. If it's even possible, it feels like he grew even bigger. Seriously, he's got to be part *Warlock* or something.

I inelegantly flop forward and accidentally take Declan with me. I'm lying face first on my pillow and he's lying on top of me. We're both panting and trying to catch our breaths.

"Can't breathe," I gripe at the suffocating wall of muscle.

He kisses my head before pulling out and rolling off of me. "Sorry," he mumbles from beside me.

I groan into my pillow. "I can't move. I think you broke me."

He opens one eye to peek out at me from his side. "Not yet, but give me like thirty minutes to recover and I'll see what I can do."

I scoff. "I don't think that I'll be able to have sex for another month after that. I think that I might have to ice my poor vagina from your pounding."

He opens both eyes and then narrows them at me. "You were the one who told me to go harder."

I roll my eyes. "Well, yeah, it seemed like a great idea at the time. Unfortunately, it's been so long that it's gotten any use, that I'm pretty sure I'll need a decent amount of time to heal."

He snorts at my words. "You have thirty minutes. Go find an ice cube or something."

I smack his arm. "I'm being serious Declan," I whine like a small child.

"So am I. And trust me when I say, that I'm a man of my word."

"These legs are closed for business for at least a week."

His grin is scary and feral again. "Challenge accepted."

And wouldn't you know? The stubborn ass man won. Not that I was complaining too much at the time.

The ringing of a phone brings wakes me out of the much-needed sleep that I was in. After round two, both Aimee and I passed out, which feels like it was only seconds ago.

I roll over and try to ignore the annoying ringing sound. To my dismay, a tiny finger pokes my side.

"Answer your damn phone, Declan, and tell whoever is on the other line, that they're soon to be dead," my little hellcat growls before pulling the blankets over her head.

I blindly reach for my phone that I placed on the bedside table earlier. I knew that I should've left the fucking thing in the living room. I continue to feel around for the device that is ruining my blissful night. Hopefully, if I don't open up my eyes, I'll fall right back asleep.

Finally, I grab the phone and crack open my right eye enough to hit the green answer button. "Someone better be dead," I growl into the phone not even bothering to check the caller ID.

"Not dead but in the ICU," my brother answers from the other line.

I sit straight up, my eyes pop open, and I am now fully awake. "Who? What happened?"

I see Aimee lower the covers through the moonlight. Her face is now a wash of concern.

"Your woman's roommate, Brad. He was found about two hours ago beat to hell. You might want to get your woman to the hospital. Looks like maybe a robbery gone wrong or something."

"Thanks, bro," I say before hanging up.

I scrub my hand down my face. I can't believe how quickly this night went from amazing to shit.

"What's wrong?" Aims asks with a quiver in her voice.

I take a deep breath and try to make sure to keep my voice as even as possible. I know damn well that she's going to freak out but I still need to try to keep her as calm as humanly possible.

I take one of her hands in my own. "Baby, we need to get over to the hospital. Damon just called me. It looks like Brad was in a robbery or something and was beaten up pretty badly."

Her gasp is loud in the otherwise quiet room. "Is he okay?" she asks. I watch as she jumps out of bed, turns on the light switch and starts rummaging around for clothes.

I take a moment to let my eyes adjust to the sudden brightness before getting up and getting dressed as well. "It's pretty bad baby. Dam said that he's in the ICU."

"Fuck," is her reply before dressing in record time.

We are both dressed, out the door, and in my truck driving to the hospital in under ten minutes.

Aimee is sitting in the passenger seat biting her nails while staring aimlessly out the window. I'm probably breaking a whole slew of traffic laws but I couldn't really give a shit at this point.

I look over at the woman that I'm pretty sure that I'm in love with and feel like I've been sucker-punched when I see the tears rolling down her face. I need to keep her busy until we get to the hospital and we can hopefully see him.

"Hey, baby?" I ask in a gentle voice.

She sniffles and wipes her cheeks before looking over at me. "Yeah?"

"Is there anyone that you should call? His family or Stacey maybe?"

She nods. "I'll call Stacey. His jerkoff family pretty much disowned him for being gay, so they can kiss my ass. I'm pretty sure that they aren't even listed as his emergency contact either," she says while taking her phone out and pressing what I assume is Stacey's number.

I remain quiet as she talks to Stacey and just keep speeding us along. Luckily at three o'clock in the morning, the streets are completely deserted. We're actually pulling into the parking lot when she hangs up.

"Stacey was just about to call me. She's already here since Brad made her his emergency contact years ago."

I park and we both make a mad dash towards the building. Aimee uses her ID badge to get us into the building and up onto the ICU floor. I'm guessing that Stacey told her what room Brad is in when they spoke since she bypasses the nurse's station.

A few of the nurses seem to give her a sympathetic glance. That doesn't exactly bode well. Dammit.

She stops at the entrance to one of the rooms and takes a deep breath before opening the door. Her gasp and the look of horror marring her beautiful face will haunt me for a long time.

When I walk in behind her and see what made that look, my stomach sinks like a stone.

Brad is completely unrecognizable and it has nothing to do with all of the wires that are coming out of him from every direction. His face looks like it was beaten with a meat tenderizer. There isn't one centimeter that isn't swollen and purple.

His left arm and right leg are in full casts. His head is bandaged so much that I'm actually afraid to ask. He has a tube coming out of his mouth. I'm guessing that's what's breathing for him at this point.

Jesus! I've never seen anyone beaten this fucking badly during a robbery. A few hits? Sure. But nothing like this. I don't want to say it out loud, but my gut is telling me that this wasn't a simple robbery. In my mind, I conclude that this looks personal but I don't voice these thoughts.

From past cases, I know that It takes a long time to beat someone this badly. Time and a lot of rage. I would bet my left nut that Brad knows the person who did this to him.

I walk into the room fully and shut the door behind me. I look over at the side of his bed and see the girls hugging and crying quietly. They're both sitting in one of those big recliner chairs that has been provided.

I take a seat in one of the other smaller chairs in the room beside Brad's bed.

Stacey looks over at me with red-rimmed eyes and gives me a sad smile. She sniffles and blows her nose before she says anything. "The police called me and said that they found him in the back of the bar's parking lot." She hiccups. "I guess one of the bar's patrons saw him when they were leaving and called the police. I just can't believe that someone would do this to him for some money."

Aimee wraps her arms around her friend even tighter. "What are we looking at?" Aimee asks sounding very much like the in-control nurse that I know her to be.

Stacey looks down at Brad and shakes her head sadly. "Well, besides the obvious broken bones, he has a few broken ribs. One that punctured his lung, hence the chest tube and breathing tube. Contusions over more than ninety percent of his body. A hairline fracture on his skull. The doctor is keeping him in a medically induced coma until the swelling comes down. We won't know about his cognitive function until he wakes up. Lacerations on his kidneys and the doctor isn't sure if they'll have to remove his spleen. Honestly, there might be more but I was in too much of a daze when he told me."

"Fuuuuck, this is a total mess," Aimee groans before taking what looks to be a calming breath. "But it doesn't matter. He's alive and that's the most important thing right now. His recovery is going to suck but at least he's alive to recover."

"Yeah," Stacey agrees in a small voice. "I just hope they find who did this to him. I seriously hope that they rot in hell for hurting someone as loving as him."

The girls go back to keeping a silent vigil at Brad's side. I lean back as far as I can in my chair and close my eyes. I try to get some rest, knowing that it's going to be hard to come by for a while.

That's exactly how Damon and Marc find me the next morning, or rather a few hours later.

I open my eyes at the knock on the door and I'm not even a little surprised seeing them enter. They're also carrying what smells to be coffee and a bunch of baked treats from Mellie and Shell's shop, *The Sweet Grind.* I could kiss these two just for the coffee alone right now.

"Here," Damon says while handing me a cup of liquid gold. "Figured that you might need this."

I raise my eyebrow with a smirk and Dam just rolls his eyes. "Fine, the girls told us that you all could use this and sent us over with it," he grumbles, sounding exactly like the grumpy bear my sister-in-law insists that he is.

"How are Aimee and Stacey doing?" Marc asks in a low voice so that he doesn't wake them up. He hands me a chocolate-filled croissant with a look of disgust. "You're turning into such a chick."

I grab the flaky goodness and take a huge bite. I moan at the fact that the croissant is still warm and the chocolate is nice and gooey. "Don't act like you don't like these too. I've seen you sneak some when you thought no one was looking."

"Yeah but I don't advertise that fact that I'm growing a vagina like you do every time you drool over the fucking things. What's next? A fucking latte?"

"Don't talk shit about those," Damon says while taking a bite of his donut. "Those mocha ones are on point."

I finish up my treat and make sure that I lick all the chocolate off my fingers. These things are so bad for my abs but are great for my taste buds.

I look up at Marc when I realize that he hasn't said anything and see him looking at us in horror. "What?" I question before taking a sip of my coffee.

He blinks a few times before responding. "What has happened to the two of you? It's like I'm losing my badass best friends. In their place are pansified versions. What happened to the guys who wouldn't even think twice about stalking someone and pushing them in front of a car with me? I want my friends back," he pouts ridiculously.

"Now who's sounding like a chick?" Dam asks in a mocking tone.

I nod my head in agreement. "Seriously, overdramatic much?"

Marc narrows his eyes at us. "It's probably happening from being around you two. Thanks to you two, the whole team will probably be nothing but a bunch of pussies soon. We'll probably even start hugging people instead of shooting them," he hisses.

The three of us turn our heads at the sounds of two tiny snorts. Admittedly, I forgot all about the girls during Marc's little tantrum. I look over and see them smiling at us.

"You guys are worse than women," Aimee retorts.

Marc and Damon cross their arms over their chests. "Yeah, how so?" Marc asks and Dam nods along.

Aimee and Stacey give each other a look. Aims sits up and leans forward in the chair that she and Stacey are still sharing. "Well, for starters, women don't go around complaining that no one will play with them anymore."

"I wasn't complaining that they wouldn't play with me," Marc mutters.

Stacey's eyes go wide while she nods her head. "Yeah, no what you were complaining about them not partaking in any longer is way worse." She gives him a grimace. "And honestly a little disturbing since you are all police officers talking about shooting people instead of hugging them."

Aimee's eyes go all squinty. "Yeah, did you guys actually push Michelle's ex in front of a car? Not all of the stories I've heard match."

The three of us look at each other with wary looks before Marc and I answer almost at the same time. "It was an accident," I say right before Marc states. "It was an act of God."

The girls blink at us and then look at Damon who just shrugs. "He was an asshole."

Stacey's mouth drops open. "He died?" She raises her hands to her mouth.

Damon takes a sip from his cup. "Unfortunately, no, he's still around."

Aimee raises an eyebrow. "Are cops supposed to say things like that? Aren't you supposed to protect people?" She stands and stretches out.

"He's kidding," I say and give a fake chuckle.

"And I'm sure that a lot of other cops are just like us. They're probably just better at hiding it," Marc supplies unhelpfully.

The girls look at each other and then back at us. "Ahhhh....."

Marc claps his hands and walks over to the girls who are looking at him like he's a weird science experiment. "Here," he says while handing them their coffees and baked goods. "My sisters thought that you might need this."

"And you just do their bidding?" Aimee's lips twitch.

Marc looks down at her with a nasty look and rubs the back of his head. "Yeah, well, they can be evil little shit heads when they want to be. They go spewing crap to my mom, who then refuses to make me her double fudge chocolate cake for family dinner night. That then pisses off my wife who is a big fan of that cake and then I have to go home with a mad wife and kids. It's just easier to do what they want some days."

"You guys are the strangest people that I've ever met," Stacey states while shaking her head.

There's a knock at the door before any of us has a chance to reply. In walks a nurse who appears to be in her mid-twenties.

"Hey Kealy," Aimee says with a little wave.

Kealy gives the girls a small smile and us guys wide berth. Not that I can blame her. The three of us don't look overly friendly. "Hey, are you two doing okay?" she asks while looking back at us as she enters the room fully.

Stacey swipes her hand in the air. "Don't worry about them. They're harmless. This one," she points to me, "is Aimee's man, Declan. That's obviously his twin, Damon, and that's Marc."

Kealy gives a tiny smile and a small wave. "Hi."

The three of us nod at her and Damon and Marc move behind me, giving her even more space.

You can just tell that being around large men freaks her out. My guess is that her past isn't overly happy with the haunted look in her eyes whenever she glances at one of us.

Kealy walks towards Brad and starts checking machines and typing something into a tablet. When she's done, she gently rubs the back of Brad's hand and sniffles.

She looks at the girls. "Did they find whoever did this to him?"

Aimee and Stacey shake their heads no. "Not yet. Hopefully, they will soon though," Aimee says sadly.

"Well, I'm on shift all day. Just let me know if you need anything. Also, be warned that he's probably going to be getting a decent number of visitors.

Everyone is so upset that something like this happened to such a sweetheart," Kealy says before walking towards the door and pulling it open.

"We will, thanks Kealy," Aimee says with a small smile before Kealy walks out and shuts the door behind her.

"Alright, well we need to get going and get to the station on time," Marc states. "You coming in or do you want us to tell them that you won't be in today?"

I look over at Aimee who waves me off. "Go on into work Dec. We're just going to be sitting around here doing nothing all day. I'll give you a call if anything changes."

I get out of the chair that I called my bed for the past few hours. It sounds and feels like every bone in my body cracks in the process. Everyone in the room is looking at me with varying degrees of disgust.

I put my arms out at my sides. "What do you all expect? I'm not exactly young anymore. I can't be sleeping in a chair like that without some repercussions."

Stacey gives me a weird look. "You should start taking better vitamins or something. I'm pretty sure that skeletons have more cushion in their joints than you do," she says while crossing her arms over her chest.

I just blink blankly at her. I'm never able to tell if she's being serious or not.

"They have some really great men's multivitamins these days. I can give you a few recommendations if you want," she says while smiling sweetly at me. Never mind, I have my answer.

"Thanks for the offer Stace, but I'm good," I reply.

She just shrugs and picks up her coffee. "Suit yourself."

Dam and Marc cough what suspiciously sounds like a laugh but say nothing. This isn't their first time near Stacey. And to be honest, she really is too sweet to ever make fun of. Unfortunately for me, that won't stop these two idiots once we're alone.

I walk over to Aimee, whose eyes are dancing with humor. I can tell that she's biting her lip so that she doesn't laugh. I just shake my head and give her a wary smile.

When I reach her, she wraps her arms around my waist and places her head on my chest. I wrap my arms around her and rest my chin on the top of her head. "You sure you don't want me to stay?" I mumble.

She tilts her head back to look at me and smiles. "No babe, I appreciate the offer but really, we'll be okay. No sense of you sitting here bored and uncomfortable. I wouldn't want you to have to start using *Icy Hot.*"

It takes me a minute to realize what she just said. "Seriously?" I drawl while looking down at her.

She gives me a sheepish look and shrugs. "I couldn't help myself. I saw the opening and I went for it."

"You're lucky that you're hot," I mumble and kiss the top of her head. I can feel her shaking with laughter. "I'll check in on you in a few," I say before stealing one more kiss and walking out the door.

Several hours later:

It's now the end of a long-ass shift and I'm sitting at a desk watching the surveillance footage from last night. There are some days that I really hate being right. Brad wasn't just beat up, it was a whole ass-kicking with multiple people. The poor guy didn't stand a chance against five other men.

I'll give it to Brad though, he held out for a long-ass time. He definitely didn't take this shit quietly. At least two of the guys have broken noses and probably a few cracked ribs. Who knew such a laid-back guy had it in him?

"This definitely wasn't a robbery gone bad," Morris states while looking over my shoulder with the rest of the guys.

"No, it wasn't." Marc leans over me and points his finger at the screen. "Rewind back to the beginning." I do as I'm told. "See here?' He points to a few dark shadows on the screen. "They were waiting for him. Look at the time stamp. They waited close to forty minutes. This was not random at all."

"Who's the guy that Brad is walking out with?" Rocco asks while also leaning over my shoulder.

I shrug my shoulders to get all of them to ease off. "Would it kill you guys to pull up a fucking chair instead of practically sitting in my damn lap and breathing on me?"

"Someone's pissy today," JJ says with a smirk.

"I'm not pissy," I huff. "I just don't need you assholes climbing all over me when there are plenty of chairs for you to sit in."

They all just blink at my outburst but thankfully go and get themselves some chairs.

"I'm guessing that you didn't use any of that *Icy Hot* that your woman so sweetly suggested," Marc states with a shit-eating grin.

I grit my teeth and pray for patience or an air-tight alibi. "No," I growl.

He purses his lips. "Maybe you should've. You might not be being such a whiny bitch right now if you had."

"I regret making sure that your kids didn't stab you," I deadpan while staring the jackass straight in the eyes.

His eyes narrow and he mumbles more to himself than to anyone else, "They love me and wouldn't have done that."

All of us just give him a side-eyed look because we're all pretty sure that they would've. Abby looked like she was one comment away from asking us to hide his body.

"Why don't we just get back to Rocco's question?" my twin growls out in his normal tone.

I shrug. "My guess would be his date. He said that he was meeting up with some guy that he met on the dating app that he's been using. Although, judging by how he joins in, I'm guessing that this whole night was premeditated."

I internally cringe as I watch Brad get beaten to within an inch of his life again. The look of utter betrayal on his face when his "date" jumps in, is something that I can never unsee. This poor guy has already gone through hell with his family and now he has to deal with this bullshit. I swear to God, when I find these motherfuckers, I'm making sure to get in a few *accidental* hits before I put their asses in cuffs.

"Jesus, they really aren't playing around," Rocco says with disgust lacing every word. "I think if that couple hadn't come out just then, that they would've killed him."

We all grunt in agreement. That couple literally saved his life by the looks of it. The twenty-something female started screaming just as one of the men were about to bring their foot down onto his head. I have no doubt that it would've killed Brad after everything else his body already suffered.

"Have we gotten any hits on who these assholes might be?" JJ asks in full business mode with his arms crossed against his chest.

"Not yet," Morris replies before cringing as we see the couple rush over to Brad and see his head flop uselessly to the side, with blood gushing from his head wound.

"I just don't get the motive for this," Marc states with a contemplative look on his face.

"They're assholes," Dam grunts.

Marc nods his head slowly at my always eloquent twin. "Yeah, they are." He leans forward, resting his arms on the tops of his thighs. "But this." He points to the screen that I've paused. "This is pure hatred. These guys hate

Brad. But I can't understand why. I've only met him a few times, but he didn't strike me as someone who would have a lot of enemies if any at all. Hell, even Damon tolerates him better than he does most people."

We all snicker at the middle finger that Dam sends Marc's way. But he's right, even my antisocial brother, who dislikes almost everyone he meets, likes Brad. So, who could actually hate him enough to do something this heinous to him?

And like I've been struck by a bolt of lightning, it comes to me. "Son of a bitch!" I hiss out in disgust. "I know who hates him but I can't actually believe that they would have this done to him."

"Who?" Morris asks.

"His family, more specifically his parents."

The guys just stare at me with varying degrees of disbelief. Damon's even giving me a dubious look. "You sure?" he asks me with a raised bushy eyebrow. Seriously, I need to talk to Shell about keeping him well-groomed.

"A hundred percent? No. But my gut is saying that they had a very large part in this."

Rocco is giving me a contemplative look. "I just can't see someone's parents doing this or having this done to their own child. I would die and kill for mine. I just can't see it."

"Unfortunately, not everyone is meant to be a parent," Marc states while leaning back in his chair.

"He has a point," Morris agrees. "I mean look at him," he says while pointing to his brother-in-law. "He loves those four little terrors with everything in him. Hell, he still doesn't realize how close he came to death by sassy toddler because he's blinded by his love for them. He would do anything for any of them. Being a great parent doesn't always mean being the one who shares DNA with them. Sometimes the shittiest parents are the ones who made you."

"They love me," Marc mumbles petulantly with his arms crossed. "They never would've done anything." Denial seems to be working out well for him.

Morris is staring at him with his mouth agape. "Really? That's all you took away from what I just said?"

Marc looks over and blinks at him. "What did you expect? For me to shed a tear and give you a hug? Jesus man, my sister has turned your ass into a damn whiny little girl."

"We really should've let those kids get some revenge," Morris says in a huff.

Rocco shakes his head sadly. "We all agreed with that. Declan is the one who killed everyone's fun."

JJ smirks at the look of shock on Marc's face from his spot against the wall. "I don't know why you look so surprised. Dec is literally the only reason you aren't at the very least missing patches of hair."

Everyone turns to look at me and I raise my hands in surrender. "Don't give me those looks. You all had women at home," Rocco raises his hand and I swipe it away. "you at least know how to cook." He shrugs and just resumes staring at me. "Mom and Kayla were my only tickets to home-cooked meals before Aimee and mom lives too far away to go over all the time. I figured Kayla wouldn't feed me anymore if something happened to him. So fucking sue me, you greedy assholes."

"You guys are seriously the world's worst friends," Marc pouts.

"Shut up," Damon growls. "You're worse than all of us combined." Ehh, he does have a point there. We're angels compared to Marc's evil ass.

Marc nods his head slowly while giving us all a weird look. "Yeah, but that's my thing. It's to be expected at this point. All of you traitors are just plain mean."

JJ scrubs his ink-covered hands up and down his face and mumbles, "I cannot believe that this is the team that I actually chose to lead. What the hell was I thinking?"

I scratch the side of my head. "Are you actually asking us or...?"

He blinks at me a few times with his lip raised in a sneer. "Hey Declan, do me a favor?"

I raise my eyebrows. "What's up boss?"

"Pull your bottom lip over your head...and swallow," he says calmly while getting a round of chuckles from the dopes surrounding us.

"Well, that's just incredibly rude and just a crappy joke. I expected better from you, but I guess at your age, lame jokes are all you really have left." I shrug with an innocent-looking smile.

"Can we get back to the issue at hand here?" Damon drawls while pointing to the screen.

He's such a damn buzzkill some days. I mean he's right, obviously, but still a damn killjoy.

"Right." I look around at my friends. "Any suggestions?"

JJ lowers his head in what almost looks like shame. "I can't believe that I'm actually saying this," he mumbles and now the rest of us are definitely all ears. Saying something like that means that the rest of us will most likely be having some fun.

"What was that?" Marc asks while giddily rubbing his hands together.

I'm not going to lie, I'm not really any better right now. I have my fingers steepled together so that I don't do the same.

We all lean forward, some of us literally on the edge of our seats waiting for JJ's next words. "The detectives are handling the case." Well, that's a bit of a letdown. "But I know how much he means to Aimee, therefore how much he means to Declan." All ears again!

JJ blows out a deep breath and places his hands on his hips while shaking his head. "I suppose that a few of you could use some of your old 'watchful' tricks and just take a look at his parents." Did he really just say what I think he did?

JJ raises his right index finger. "But." Dammit. "None of you are to interact with them in any way, shape, or form. Do you understand me?" He looks at all of us with a look that could peel paint. "So help me God, nothing bad better happen. I fucking mean it you three." He points to Marc, Dam, and myself. "There better be no 'accidents' or 'karma' or whatever bullshit you three have tried to feed me."

"Act of God," I helpfully reply.

The scowl I receive from JJ is honestly quite impressive. "Nothing! Do you hear me?"

We all nod our heads like the obedient children that I doubt any of us ever were.

"I mean it!" he growls well enough to give Damon a run for his money.

"Don't worry." I swipe a hand through the air. "What's the worst that can happen from watching someone?"

They all look over at me in horror. "Did you actually just say that?" Morris asks with a terrified look on his face.

I just shrug. "Ehh, it'll be fine, you'll see." I really fucking hope that's true.

The past few weeks have been a whirlwind of emotions. Some good and a lot bad. It took over four days for the swelling on Brad's brain to go down. Four days of one of my best friends being in a medically induced coma. To say that those days went by like years is an understatement.

Luckily, once Brad was awake, his doctors ran a bunch of cognitive tests and MRI's. Everything came back completely normal, which is a miracle considering what he went through. The rest of his body, well, that was still damaged to hell.

Now we all know that men make the worst patients. Add in the fact that the patient is also a nurse and you have a recipe for disaster. Someone was not a happy camper when the doctors told him that he would be spending at least a week there. Honestly, he threw such a large hissy fit that he would make any toddler proud.

His lung healed up nicely and was able to have the chest tube removed fairly quickly. Even better he was able to keep his spleen but bitched about peeing blood due to the lacerations on his kidneys. I'm not even going to get into how much he complained about his damn casts.

You would think that the bone head didn't almost die with the way he complained about everything under the sun. He also freaked the hell out when Stacey and I tried to help him get dressed.

Apparently, we are to never see him naked. Because we're not nurses and haven't seen twigs and berries a million times before. He also didn't really appreciate us calling his manhood that. He even had Declan give us a long lecture on how we are to never use that term again.

Declan and surprisingly Damon have been a godsend. They had no problem stepping in when Brad needed to get dressed or be helped to the bathroom. Declan even helped Brad wash up over the past few weeks.

I'm pretty sure that Brad is even more in love with Declan than I am at this point. I'm kidding...well sort of. I swear, he has Brad's undying devotion now.

And dammit if watching him help my best friend like it's nothing didn't make me give up that little piece of my heart that I had been holding back. Even Damon now has a special place in my heart, that I'm one thousand percent positive we will never need to talk about.

Everyone has stopped by at one point or another, even Kayla's family members and Sage's ex. Which if I'm being honest, I still haven't figured out how all of that works but whatever. Danny has decided to make it his mission in life to teach Brad how to *kick ass like a mother fucker.* I think we're all extremely happy about that, to be honest.

"Will you stop scratching!" I yell at the man-child who is currently lying on our couch sticking a hanger down his cast.

"It itches," he whines pathetically.

I walk over and snatch the hanger out of his hand. "Knock it off. You're going to end up cutting yourself. You know damn well that your skin is paper-thin under that thing right now. The last thing we need is you bleeding under that cast."

Seriously, he freaking sharpened the plastic end into a damn point. I get that the cast itches after wearing it for the past five weeks, but Jesus, he's being a little extreme.

"I can't wait to get these things off!" he grumbles while giving me a nasty look that I'm nice enough to ignore.

I know that he's miserable. Soon enough, he'll be healed up and back to normal...hopefully. Physically, he'll be healed soon. Mentally, well, I think that's going to take some time.

A part of the old Brad died that night. He hasn't been his happy-go-lucky self since. Not that I can really blame him. Especially after what he told us those guys said while they were hitting him.

I never imagined that someone could hate someone else so much just because of their sexual orientation. But, my God, the things he told us that they said. Stacey and I cried like babies while Brad just sat there stoically replaying every word.

"You only have another week for your arm." I try to console.

"I know. But I still have at least another three weeks for my leg," he states miserably.

I walk over and toss the hanger into the trash can in the kitchen. I look over my shoulder and give him a winning smile. "Hey, at least you're not also still recovering from having your spleen removed. Things could always be worse," I chirp just to be a little annoying. What? It's been a long few weeks.

My normally vibrant friend looks washed out among his sea of blankets and pillows. He's lost so much weight recently that he's beginning to look a little gaunt. I need to start feeding him some calorie-laden snacks and meals.

His head drops back onto his pillow. "I know that you're right." He sighs heavily. "It just sucks not being able to move or do anything for myself."

I walk over and take a seat on the edge of one of his cushions. I pat his arm reassuringly. "I know honey. Just a few more weeks and you'll be back to your annoyingly active self."

He wraps his good arm around me and nuzzles his head onto me. "Thank you for taking such good care of me. I'm sorry that I've been such a miserable asshole." His voice mumbled from where he's snuggled up.

I run my hand through his hair that is definitely two days overdue for a wash. "It's okay. I know that you don't really mean it. You're a man, you're all whiny bitches when it comes to being sick," I say cheekily and receive a snort in reply.

"I wish that I could disagree with you."

"But you can't," I say before muttering, "Unfortunately."

He looks up at me with sad puppy dog eyes. "I really am sorry that I've been such a shit."

I just shrug. "It's all good in the hood."

He blinks and then blinks some more. "Why would you ever say that?" he asks with a voice laced with disgust.

I raise my hands in surrender. "Sage said it and now it's still on my mind."

Brad nods thoughtfully. "Yeah, but even the three girls told her to stop saying that. I know that we're all getting older, but you're not old enough to say shit that lame. I know that you've been too busy to cover up some of that gray hair recently, but it's like you're not even trying anymore."

I purse my lips. "Has it occurred to you not to piss off one of the people that you're currently relying on for everything?"

"Nah, I figure Declan will save me," he replies casually and I roll my eyes.

"Please. Declan likes getting laid. He'll let me do whatever I want to you as long as he gets sexy time."

He quirks an eyebrow and gets a mischievous look on his face that has been missing lately. "Considering what the hair on top of your head has looked like lately, I can only imagine the disaster that you've got going on down south. Dec might just thank me for interrupting sexy time." I narrow my eyes at the jerk. "The poor guy probably already deserves a medal," he mutters...just not low enough.

116

"I'm literally going to put peroxide in your hair when you're asleep so that you wake up looking like a nineties boyband reject," I say calmly.

He lies back on his pillow and scowls up at me. "If you do that, once I'm healed, I'm going to rip up every pair of leggings that you own."

I lower my face so that we're nose to nose, both of us ignoring the sound of the front door opening and closing. "You do that and I will gut you," I hiss.

"Try it and your ugly ass Uggs will be next."

"Ahem." We both look up at the amused sounding voice. "Am I interrupting anything?" Declan asks with a grin.

I bat my lashes at him. "I was just explaining to Brad what would happen if he messed with my leggings and Uggs," I say sweetly.

Never one to be outdone, Brad chimes in, "And I was just explaining to Aims that you deserve a medal for still wanting to tap her rachet looking ass."

I look over at the sound of more than one masculine chuckle and realize that Declan isn't alone. Nope, he's brought Damon and Marc home with him. Just kill me now! My face feels like it's a three-alarm fire. Once Brad's all better, I'm going to kill him!

I smile and give an awkward wave. "Hi, guys."

I get a head nod and I'm pretty sure a lip twitch from Damon and a "Hey Aims," through a chuckle from Marc. Yup, definitely killing my roommate when he's all healed up.

Declan strolls into the living room with a grin on his obnoxiously handsome face.

I get off the couch and step away from the traitor that I live with. I walk into Declan's open arms and squeeze him. I swear that he gives the world's best hugs. There hasn't been anything that one of his hugs couldn't make better.

117

I inhale deeply, loving the smell of his cologne mixed in with his unique scent. I can feel his body shaking. I tilt my head back to look up at him. "What are you laughing at?" I question.

"Are you sniffing me again?"

I roll my eyes because this isn't a new conversation. I can't help it. His smell is like catnip to me or something. And he knows damn well that I was sniffing him.

"You know that I was," I say primly.

"Women are so strange," Declan says.

"Doll does it all the time."

"Kayla too."

His buddies agree.

I lean around my man and stare at the other two. "What are you guys doing here again?"

Marc clutches his chest with a fake hurt expression. "I can't believe that you would ask that. Of course, we're here to see your pleasant self." He looks over at Brad with a wicked gleam in his eye. "Or was that your 'rachet self' as Brad said."

"Ass. I said rachet ass," Brad ever so helpfully replies.

My lips thin. "You guys realize, that as a woman, that I can be decently petty...right?"

"What's that supposed to mean hellcat?" Declan asks warily while walking towards the fridge, my guess in search of the beer that I now keep stocked for him.

I smile sweetly at the four men that are pressing their luck. "Nothing." I shrug casually. "I'm just making conversation."

"Making conversation my ass," Brad mutters.

I look down with a raised eyebrow. "What was that?"

"I love you so much. You're the world's best and prettiest roommate," he says like a man who just realized that he needs me.

"That's what I thought," I say while walking towards the island and taking a seat at the counter.

I look at the three men standing in my kitchen and realize that they are all dressed alike. Black shirts, black hats, dark blue jeans, and black boots. Huh, that's odd.

"Why you lookin' at us like that?" Damon questions with his head tilted.

Declan hands me a glass of wine. "Thanks, babe," I reply before turning back to Damon. "I'm just trying to figure out if ya'll meant to dress like that or if it was just a happy accident since you spend so much time together."

Later on, I would look back on the funny way they looked at each other and realize that something wasn't quite right. I really should've paid more attention to the side-eyed look that they gave each other, but it was a long week...and wine.

"Huh? I guess we did dress the same," Declan says in an odd tone that I ignore in favor of drinking my wine.

"Maybe you guys shouldn't spend so much time together if you're starting to dress the same."

Marc blinks at me and then gives me a megawatt smile. "You're probably right." He nods his head.

"Are you okay?" I ask Declan in concern.

He finishes coughing/choking on the sip of beer he just took. "Fine," he gasps while hitting his chest. "Just went down the wrong pipe."

I give him a dubious look. "You sure?"

He smiles. "Yup, all better now."

"Ah, okay. Well, I'm going to go take a bath. I have lobster mac and cheese baking in the oven. If you could take it out when the timer goes off, I'd really appreciate it." I say to no one in particular since I'm pretty sure that Marc and Damon are staying for dinner.

"How much did you make?" Marc asks trying and failing nonchalance.

I roll my eyes. "Enough for you two to eat as well," I say while refilling my wine glass.

"Have I ever told you how happy I am for you and Declan?"

"You're just happy to have someone else to mooch a meal off of when Kayla is working."

Leaning his back against the counter, legs crossed at the ankle and with a beer bottle in his hand, Marc looks way too comfortable here. "It's only fair since Dec practically lived with us for a while."

"I was being a good friend and saving your life," Declan mumbles while rummaging through the cabinets.

"What are you doing?" I ask the sexy man that I get to call mine.

He looks over his shoulder at me. "Looking for a snack."

I blink. "I just told you that dinner was in the oven."

"Yeah, but the timer says that there's still thirty-six minutes left. I need something to hold me over."

"Dinner is in a half an hour," I reply blandly.

"I know."

We just stare at each other blankly. I finally snap out of it. "Whatever. Ruin your dinner, not my problem." I shrug.

"I feel like that was a bit passive-aggressive," he says like a moron.

"Why would I be passive-aggressive about the fact that I made lobster mac and cheese from scratch and thirty minutes before we eat, you're looking for a snack?"

"Is this a trick question?" His tone is unsure while eyeing me warily.

"You really should shut up," Damon grumbles.

"Shh, let him keep going. I want to see what happens," Marc says while his eyes keeping bouncing between Declan and me.

I turn my head in their direction. "Don't you two have anything better to do than stand here and listen to us?"

"No," they answer in unison.

I take a deep breath and then say "screw it" mentally. I not only grab my wine glass but the rest of the bottle as well. "I'll be in the bathtub if any of you need me. But I'm telling you right now, that you better not need me."

With that parting remark, I walk calmly down the hall and walk into my bedroom. Before I close the door, I hear. "I'm guessing that I shouldn't have a snack, huh?" I just shut the door before I hear anyone's reply.

Several days later:

Do you know what everyday life doesn't prepare you for? Finding out that your boyfriend is currently getting yelled at by the chief of police for stalking your roommate's parents. I can't even believe that that sentence is even a thing in my life.

Granted, when I met Declan, I realized that my days would most likely never be boring. I mean come on, he's a riot and a very loveable goofball. Sure, he's mischievous but it's all in good fun. Usually at Marc or Kayla's expense.

So, I really had no idea that I would be blindsided by the fact that he was in trouble for stalking. The worst part is, this isn't even the first time. Even worse, is that no one else even seems remotely surprised or upset. Well, besides the chief of police who is screaming at the guys in his office.

Seriously, everyone in what I was told is called the *"ball pen"* has stopped what they're doing and are just listening to the ass chewing going on. Not that I can blame them since I'm doing the same damn thing. But damn, the entire police station has gone silent.

"How bad do you think it is?" Lavender asks while worrying her bottom lip.

Mellie gives a little shrug. "No one's in the hospital. I'm sure it's fine."

Shell nods her head in agreement. "Yeah, this isn't bad at all."

"Totally could've been worse," Kayla agrees.

Sage, Lavender and I just stare at them with our mouths open. They can't be serious. But I have a funny feeling that they are. None of them look overly concerned. I've actually caught Mellie looking at the time on her phone in annoyance a few times.

"I wonder how much longer this is going to take?" Mellie asks no one in particular while looking at her phone yet again. "We were supposed to leave for dinner twenty minutes ago. I'm starving. I purposely skipped lunch so that I wouldn't feel guilty about all the tacos and margaritas that I plan on having."

We're all here at the station because us girls drove in together so that we wouldn't have too many cars at dinner. We figured that we would come here and get the guys, and then go to dinner. Hence, why we are sitting here listening to our men get reamed out.

"Ah, I know! I'm freaking starving. Mason is carb-loading or some bullshit and ate my sandwich today," Kayla tells us.

Michelle looks around Mellie towards Kayla. "Why carbs? Isn't that the opposite of what someone going to the gym needs?" she asks seemingly very curious.

Kay smacks her gum and shrugs. "I have no idea. Something about bulking or getting bigger. I completely spaced out when he was telling me."

"Seriously, is no one else concerned that the guys are in there getting screamed at?" I ask anyone.

Sage and Lav raise their fingers while the other three just lift a shoulder. Dear Lord, I don't know who's worse, them or the guys.

"I'm going to go see if I can get something to drink. Anyone want anything?"

They all respond with a "no" or a shake of their heads. I get up out of my chair and walk towards the front. They have to have a soda machine or something in this place. As I'm walking, I see a blonde woman sitting at the reception desk and figure that I might as well ask her.

I walk to the front of the desk and give the woman a smile that earns me a nasty scowl. Umm, well okay then. "Excuse me?"

This chick actually rolls her damn eyes at me. "Yeah?"

Deep breaths Aims. Just act like she's another one of your annoying ass patients who think that they're dying because they have a freaking splinter.

I just smile even brighter at her. "Could you please tell me where I would be able to get something to drink.?"

"At one of the stores or restaurants on the block," she says rudely.

What in the hell is her issue? "They don't have anywhere for me to get something to drink here? In the entire police station? Not even a drinking fountain?"

She looks up at me with what I'm sure she's hoping is a mean glare. But it loses its fierceness since her makeup is caked on so badly that you can't really tell what expression she's supposed to be making. Hell, her eyebrows are constantly raised since she drew them on that way. "Only for the officers. Sorry," she says insincerely with a fake ass smile.

"Thanks," I growl out mean enough to make Damon proud.

I stomp back over to my seat and see the rest of the girls smirking at me. I flop back down into my seat and cross my arms. I start tapping my foot since what I really want to do is a bad idea with so many police officer witnesses. "What in the hell is Barbie-wannabe's problem?"

I hear a few snorts and Mellie leans forward in her chair. "You've never had the displeasure of dealing with Deanna I'm guessing."

"Nope."

"Pleasant, isn't she?" Kayla chuckles to herself.

I just shake my head. "Seriously, what the hell is her damage?"

Michelle swipes a hand in the air. "Oh, she hates all of us because she thought that she was going to land one of our guys. I don't think she actually cared who, but one of them was supposed to be hers."

"Like the guys don't think that she's just as annoying as we do." Kay rolls her eyes.

"Does she hit on them?" Lavender gasps with wide eyes.

Mellie shakes her head. "No, but she's so sweet to them, that it'll give you a toothache. That bitch really needs to go already," Mellie grumbles, earning a smile from Michelle.

Sage gives them a confused look. "I just don't understand how she's so rude to everyone and doesn't get fired."

"Because her bitch ass is only ever rude to other women. She's sweet as pie to any man who will even look in her skanky ass direction," Mellie hisses like a feral cat.

All of us besides Michelle just stare at Mellie. Damn, I wouldn't put it past her to stick gum in this chick's hair or something. Actually, come to think of it, that isn't such a bad idea. Maybe it would make her get a better hairstyle.

Bleached out, frizzy hair went out in the nineties. I'd be doing her and everyone else who has to look at her a favor really.

I shake my head mentally at myself. Jesus, I have been spending way too much time with Declan. His bad habits and ideas are rubbing off on me.

"Why are you shaking your head like a wet dog?" Sage, ever so nicely asks.

"I was thinking about how it would help humanity out if I stuck gum in her hair so that no one would have to look at that awful hairstyle anymore. And then I realized that I'm spending too much time with Declan because his bad ideas are rubbing off on me," I tell them all.

I also get a little uncomfortable with the way Mellie's eyes light up like a woman who just found out that Ulta is having a sale. "Huh, I never thought of doing something like that."

"I find that hard to believe," I say before I can stop myself. Luckily, she takes absolutely no offense to what I said.

She waves a hand in the air. "Oh, don't get me wrong. I've thought about doing plenty of things to her. But that seems like an idea that would keep me out of prison."

I frown and tilt my head at her. "What were your ideas?" Though, if I'm being honest, I'm kind of frightened to actually know.

She lifts one shoulder. "Eh, nothing you need to worry about."

Yeah, that's really not comforting at all. I'm thinking that chick is one nasty remark away from an accident.

Just as I'm about to ask them something else, the office door opens and all six of the guys coming strolling out. Yes, strolling like they didn't just get yelled at or possibly fired. It's like I'm in the damn twilight zone or something.

The rest of the nosy asses in the station start shuffling around like they haven't been eavesdropping the entire time. I just shake my head, not believing that this is actually my life these days.

125

"Hey, hellcat," Declan says while smiling down at me. I just stare blankly at him. "What's wrong?"

"You ready to go?" I ask, instead of asking what the hell is going on. I figure that I have a better chance of getting him to tell me once we're alone in his truck.

He nods his head slowly like I'm some weird creature that he's never seen before. "Yeah, just let me grab my stuff. I'll be right back," he says slowly before turning around and walking towards the back of the police station. The other guys follow him.

Luckily, they all come back out in under two minutes. We all make our way out of the building and towards the parking lot. We all go our separate ways and get into our vehicles.

Declan opens my door for me and helps me in. As usual, he waits until I'm buckled up before he'll shut the door. I have no idea what his deal with my seat belt is, but I've decided it's just easier to go along with him on this one.

He gets in, buckles his own seat belt and starts the truck. He taps his fingers on the steering wheel a few times before shifting into drive and pulling out of his parking spot.

He sighs loudly. "Alright. Hit me with it. I know that you're dying over there."

I narrow my eyes and cross my arms over my chest. "What the hell were you guys doing?" I grit out.

He pulls out onto Main Street and drives a few moments. My guess is that he's collecting his thoughts and figuring out exactly how much to tell me. I just tap my foot impatiently, letting him know that my patience is thinning.

He gives me a side-eyed grimace. "Would you believe that it was a misunderstanding?" he asks hopefully.

My lips thin. "For anyone else but you six...sure," I deadpan.

"Right." He rubs his hand across his face, making that scratching sound. "How about it being a total accident?"

"I feel like you're purposely trying to piss me off by insulting my intelligence."

He lows out a big breath. "Okay, but in my defense, this was all JJ's fault."

I blink and then I blink some more while my brain tried to comprehend what he just said. "Your superior is the one at fault?" I ask dubiously, because let's be real here, JJ is the most level headed out of all of them, with Morris seeming to be a close second.

"Sort of."

"Sort of?" I raise my eyebrow.

He looks over at me and frowns. "Are you going to keep repeating everything that I say?"

"Possibly, since it's the only way to get my brain to process the bullshit that is coming out of your mouth," I answer honestly.

He holds up a finger. "Okay first, not all of it is bullshit." He makes a left turn before holding up another finger. "And secondly, that's really annoying."

"You make me want to drink...heavily." I sigh and lean my head against my window.

"That's fine. We're going to a place that has awesome margaritas that you love to drink your weight in."

I roll my head to the left to look at the moron that I call mine. "Do you ever want to actually get laid again? Or are you going to give celibacy a try?"

He gives me a sheepish smile. "You're so pretty and smart."

I roll my eyes at the dope doling out horrible compliments. I motion with my hand. "Just get on with the explanation already. We're almost there." Thank God! I really could go for a few margaritas right now.

He sucks his right cheek into his mouth and purses his lips. "Okay, so after watching the surveillance video from the night that Brad was attacked, I had a gut feeling."

"What was on the video?" I ask. I didn't know that there was one.

Dec briefly looks over at me before returning his eyes back to the road. "Everything baby. We watched the entire thing happen," he says sadly.

I gasp and cover my mouth with my hands. "So, that means you know who did it then, right?"

"Yes and no. It was really dark Aims. All we saw was four dark figures waiting for him."

I turn my head to face Declan completely. "What do you mean waiting for him? I thought that it was just a hate crime or whatever?" I rub my hands up and down my arms, suddenly getting a horrible chill.

"No baby, they were waiting specifically for him. I'm sure that a lot of hate was involved, but several other gay men came out of that bar before Brad did. And since his date was one of the guys who attacked him..."

I hold up my left hand to stop him. "What do you mean his date was one of the guys who attacked him?" I growl out.

Declan looks over at me warily. "He didn't tell you that part?"

"No, he did not."

Dec scratches the side of his neck. "Ah, well, yeah. His date brought him outside and directly towards the other four that were waiting in the shadows. They proceeded to attack him. But luckily a young couple coming out from one of the other bars saw and scared the guys away. Most likely saving Brad's life in the process."

"What does this have to do with his parents though? They're assholes...sure, but they weren't there." I ask the question but I have a bad feeling that I know the answer.

Declan parks the truck and gives me a sad smile. "Who else hates Brad enough to do something like this? No one dislikes Brad. Hell, even Damon likes him. It was the only logical thing."

Well hell, when he puts it like that...yeah it is.

I can see the moment that she realizes that his shitty ass parents were probably the ones behind this whole mess. Her expression is part sad, part pissed and part resigned.

I turn the truck off but make no effort to get out. I want to finish this conversation, that way we can hopefully enjoy a little bit of dinner tonight.

I turn to my right and drape my arm across the back of her seat. Her eyes are moving around like they do when she's really contemplating something.

She leans back against her door so that she's facing me as well. "Okay, it's totally plausible that his asshole parents had something to do with this. His dad especially. That man has a mean streak a mile wide."

I rub my chin that could use a razor at some point. "Yeah, he seems like someone who likes to pick on those that he views as weaker."

In all honesty, the guy seems like the world's biggest scumbag. It was hard as hell not to put my fist through his face, especially when I saw all the black and blue marks on his wife.

Aimee nods her head. "His sister Brooke has said as much. I know that she couldn't wait to get out of the house."

I look at her in alarm. "He has a sister?" Christ, his wife is one thing. She's making a choice to stay, but I'll be damned if I sit by while someone with no choice is harmed.

She gives me a small smile. "A younger sister," she reaches out and pats my bicep, "but don't worry, she's been away at college for the past three years. When she does come home for summer, she stays with us or Stacey. We never let her go back there."

I grind my teeth. "He hit her too, didn't he?"

"Yeah, which is why no one cares if she spends months living with us. Though, she now has an off-campus apartment, so she hasn't done that in about a year."

I feel mildly better about that. At least she's not being abused any longer.

Aimee leans her head against the headrest and gives me a wary smile. "So...out with it."

I raise an eyebrow and give her my charming smile. A man needs to use everything in his arsenal some days. "Out with what?" Playing dumb has worked for me before, might as well try it again.

Her eyes do that squinty thing that usually means I'm in trouble. "Why were you six in the chief of police's office getting screamed at? What in the hell did you dopes do?"

I raise my hands at my little hellcat in surrender. "Okay, this was seriously not my fault-" I try for another award-winning smile and mutter "-this time."

She sighs and bangs her head against the headrest a few times. "Speed this along Dec," she motions with her hands, "my thighs may be thick, but my patience is not."

With the way that she's glaring at me, I have a feeling that I'm not getting between those delightfully thick thighs for a while.

I cough into my hand and try to calm my dick down from just the thought of her. This is the wrong time to be popping up buddy, I think mentally. From the looks on her face, Mr. Right and Mr. Left will be my only companions for a bit.

I take a deep breath. "In a nutshell, JJ suggested that maybe we should put some of our former activities to good use and just check up on Brad's parents."

Aimee scrounges up her lips. "How did that end up with you all getting yelled at?" Crossing her arms, she taps her foot against the floorboard.

This is probably a bad time to tell her how sexy she looks when she's pissed off. I look at the scowl on her face again, and yup, bad time to mention it.

I tug on my right ear. "It seems that we're a tiny bit out of practice. Which is ridiculous, considering Damon and I stalked Michelle for close to two years."

Aims blinks at me a few times with her mouth open before shaking her head. "There is so much wrong with that statement."

I nod my head in agreement. "I know...right? You would think that it would be like riding a bike or some shit."

"Yeah, that's totally not what I meant," she mumbles while gripping the bridge of her nose. "Let's just forget about how possibly disturbed you are for a minute." I frown at her but she ignores me. "But believe me, we will be going back to that. What actually happened? We need to get inside where the tequila is."

I tilt my head at her. "I'm beginning to think that you have a drinking problem."

"I'm beginning to think that you're the cause of it," she says without any hesitation.

"Anyway," I narrow my eyes at the woman that I might have to admit to the Betty Ford Clinic for alcohol abuse treatment, "It basically comes down to them realizing that we were around too much. Then a verbal sparring match

132

happened. Some threats thrown in and them making a call to the Chief. All in all, not our best work, but not our worst either." I shrug.

Judging by the look on my poor woman's face, I think that I might have broken her. She's staring at me, but there doesn't really seem to be anyone home right now.

I wave my hand in front of her face. "Babe? You okay in there?" I snap my fingers, which causes her to come to.

"How is it that trained officers and ex-military men were spotted so easily?" she asks reasonably.

I tug on my ear again. "So, you see, that part is kind of Marc's fault." I look over at her and she waves a hand for me to continue. "He kind of riled Damon up about all the men that he had to watch hit on Michelle and her go out on dates with. Dam got kind of pissed and shoved Marc. Morris and Rocco tried to break it up," I rub the back of my neck, "And needless to say we made a tiny bit of a commotion."

She's pinching the bridge of her nose. "And the arguing and threats?"

"We were already kind of keyed up and just let shit kind of fly. Like I said, not our best work."

She gives me a calculating look. "And where were you during all of that?"

"Being a good twin. I was behind Dam, ready to help him kick Marc's ass." I mean really...where else would I be?

"Let's just go inside," she sighs loudly, "I'm far too sober for this type of conversation. We'll finish It later once I have a decent buzz."

Without another word, she hops out of my truck, slams the door and power walks to the entrance.

Well, tonight should be interesting.

Several hours later and many, many margaritas consumed and yep, I was right. Tonight has been extremely interesting and entertaining.

All of our women were obviously upset with us since they drank those pitchers like it was water. I'm actually somewhat worried about their livers. Even Lavender, who doesn't really drink, drank like it was her damn job.

It was actually pretty entertaining to listen to them "whisper" about how pissed at us they were. A group of drunk women is anything but quiet. But at least we all know how they plan on making us suffer...well if they remember what they came up with anyway. Which I highly doubt, since they were all six drinks in by that point.

Getting six sloshed women out of that place was harder than going through boot camp. Nothing in life prepares you for the fight a woman can put up when you try to take away her margarita.

Also surprising was that Lavender was the feistiest out of all of them. Though, I'm not really sure why she was yelling at Rocco. Something to do with a "sweet as candy, bleached out, wannabe barbie whore." I'm pretty sure we all know who she was talking about...just not why. I mentally shrug. Whatever, not my problem.

I have enough to worry about with my own hellcat. Of course, she couldn't pass out on the way home, nope...not her. Nope, she sat in the passenger's seat with her arms crossed the entire time.

She seems hell-bent on finishing our earlier conversation, much to my dismay. Luckily, we're at my place tonight, since Stacey is staying with Brad. At least no one else will bear witness to her tirade.

And I know damn well that's exactly what it will be...a tirade. She has been shooting me daggers ever since we walked into my place ten minutes ago. She's done everything from changing into sleep clothes to taking off her makeup to brushing her teeth with an attitude.

I really shouldn't find it as sexy as I do.

I'm currently lying in bed, in only my boxers, on top of the covers, hoping that my abs will distract her when she walks in. I'm tired and have no urge to listen to her yell at me some more. I got enough of that with the Chief this afternoon.

But I'm a smart enough man to know that I need to just let her get it out if she wants. That was the one thing our dad always taught us. That it's easier to let a woman yell at you when she feels like it. It's ten times worse when she's stewed over something for days.

I hear the bathroom door open and it takes supreme effort not to smile. She is so fucking adorable without even meaning to be. She's in one of my shirts and a pair of my boxers. Her hair is up in one of those crazy ball things on the top of her head that all women wear a lot. But what's really cute is that she's trying to scowl at me with one eye closed.

Her glare loses some of its fierceness when she can only see straight with one eye. It also doesn't help that she's holding onto the wall just to walk to bed. I cover my mouth with my hand since I can't keep the smile off my face any longer.

"You okay baby?" I try to say with a minimal chuckle.

"Shut up," she growls before walking into the bedside table. "Mother fucker!" she hisses while trying to hold onto her right knee. That's probably going to leave a mark.

"Need some help?" I can't even keep the mirth out of my voice anymore.

"No," she mutters petulantly before flopping into bed. She moves around for a few seconds, obviously trying to get her bearings. She finally lands her head on her pillow and gives me a goofy, triumphant smile. "See?"

I feel like Damon with how my lips twitch. "Good job hellcat."

She stretches out with her arms above her head and sighs. "I know. I'm so awesome," she slurs.

135

What she is, is currently a mess. Not that I'm dumb enough to say that to her. I like my life, thank you very much. Nothing worse than a drunk pissed off women.

She actually reminds me of a cat in the sun with the way she is stretching. Arms up, causing her shirt and breasts to lift. Like a very happy pussy cat. Annnnd, now I'm hard.

I nonchalantly get under the covers. There's no telling how it would go if she saw my hardon right now. I know how I would want it to go, but let's face it, that probably isn't in the cards for me tonight.

I try to palm my dick a bit to get some relief. I swear Aimee has some freaky ass power over me. All I have to do is be within a hundred feet of her and I'm hard. I thought that it would get better once we had sex, but nope, it's worse. Now that my dick knows what she feels like, he wants her all the damn time.

"Do you have to pee?" I look over at the sound of her voice to see her staring at me curiously.

"No...why?" I ask.

She points to my hand that is still on top of my dick. "Because you're holding yourself like a kid who has to pee."

Or a grown-ass man who has suddenly turned into a teenager again, I think to myself.

"Nope, just like the way I feel," I blurt out before I really think about what I'm saying. All of my blood is obviously no longer in my head on top of my shoulders.

"You like the way you feel?" she asks ever so slowly.

"Yeah." In for a penny, in for a pound.

She squints at me through glassy eyes. "Right. Are you sure that you're not unbalanced or unhinged?"

I roll onto my left side so that I can look at her. "No, why do you keep asking me that?"

"No reason," she lies horribly.

She lies there for a few minutes with her lips moving like she's having a conversation with some invisible person. And she asks me if I'm unhinged, I mentally snort.

When she stops talking to herself, she rolls her head to look at me. "I want to have sex," she slur/whines.

I blink a few times but answer quickly. "I'm good with that." What man in his right mind is going to tell his woman no? Not me...that's for damn sure.

She gives me a drool look. "Of course, you are," she states blandly while rolling her pretty grey eyes at me. "But unfortunately, we can't."

I try to casually start tugging off my boxers, which is a lot harder to do when you don't want to move too much. I wouldn't want to break the spell or anything.

"No, no, don't worry, we definitely can. I'll even do all the work," I offer graciously.

In response, I get her cute little piglet snort. "As selfless as that offer is, I'm going to have to pass."

"Whhyy." It's now my turn to whine like a child.

"Because the room is still spinning, even after I just got the bed to stop. But if you want me to puke all over you, go for it."

"At least I won't have to try to sleep with a boner now," I sigh and pull my boxers back up.

"I try to be helpful like that."

"You're too kind babe," I grumble.

"I know," is the last thing that she mumbles before she passes out.

I pull the covers up to her chin and tuck her in like a human burrito, the way she likes. I kiss her right temple and breathe in her scent.

I lay my head next to hers. My last thought before sleep claims me, is that I can't believe how lucky I am.

However, the next morning, I'm not feeling so lucky. Nothing like waking up to the sound of your woman puking her guts up. I guess she really wasn't kidding last night about the whole throwing up on me thing.

Yeah, I definitely dodged a bullet there.

I grab my phone off of my nightstand and see that it's a little past nine in the morning. I look through some of the messages and text my brother back. I let him know that he's never allowed to let Michelle pour Aimee's drinks ever again.

I scrub my hand down my face to get all the sleep out of my eyes and roll until I'm on Aimee's side of the bed. I sit at the edge and stretch my arms above my head and let out a nice long sigh when my back and neck crack.

Jesus, I'm getting old if that's what feels great in the morning.

I stand up and cautiously walk towards the bathroom door. I can hear Aimee still throwing up what she ate for breakfast when she was ten.

Is it normal for someone to throw up so much?

I open the door and my heart breaks for my poor woman.

Aimee is sitting on the floor literally hugging the toilet. When she looks up at me with makeup running down her face and a greenish tint to her skin, it takes everything in me to not just pick her up and cradle her.

I lean against the doorframe and cross my arms over my chest. "You doing okay hellcat?"

She lays her head down on top of the toilet seat. "I'm never drinking again," she whimpers pathetically.

If I wasn't so sure that she would find a way to stab me, I would definitely tell her that I tried to get her to slow down. But since I don't feel like dying today, I go with, "Do you need me to get you anything?"

"A dark hole that I can crawl in and die."

I can't even help my smirk. "Anything else?"

"Ginger ale and crackers."

I knock on the door frame a few times. "You got it, baby. I'll be back in a few."

I turn and walk to the kitchen. I may not be your typical messy bachelor but I don't really keep the place too stocked. Especially since I've been spending most of my time at Aimee's because of Brad's recovery.

I open my fridge and see that it's pretty much bare except for some ketchup, mustard and oddly enough, strawberry syrup. Hmm, Aims or my mom must have put that in there.

I close the door and walk into the pantry and see that I do have crackers but no ginger ale. I look at the box of crackers and turn them over in my hand. I have no idea when I even bought these things. I look on the box for an expiration date and yup, there it is, these bad boys expired two years ago.

Damn, I really need to go through all of this shit. I'm getting as bad as some frat boy hoarder. What's next? I stop cleaning up after myself? I shake my head. I do need to spend a little bit more time sorting things out around here. I'm actually afraid to look in my freezer.

"Why do you look so disgusted?" I hear croaked from right behind me.

I jump and turn towards Aims. "Damn, I didn't hear you come in."

"Yeah, I got that from the weird-ass conversation that you seemed to be having with yourself," she states while plopping into one of the kitchen chairs.

My poor baby looks so pathetic right now. "Okay, so I have some good news and some bad news."

She has her arms on the table, cradling her head. She pops one eye open to look at me. "Okay," she says in an unsure tone.

"I have no food here." I ignore her snort. "So that's the bad news." I am also nice enough to ignore her little eye roll. "The good news is, that I am more than happy to take you out to breakfast so that you can soak up some of that tequila."

She actually gags. "Do not mention the T word right now...or ever again," she mutters. "Why can't you just go out and get some food, while I stay here and die in peace?"

I walk up to her with my boyish grin and wrap my arms around her. I pull her out of the chair and steady her on her feet. I put her face in between my hands and get nose to nose with her. "Because I love you and want to spend the whole day with you, even if you're going to be miserable and cranky the entire time."

I feel her go solid and figure that she's trying to come up with a way out of it. I gently shove her towards the door and give her a little pat on her perfect ass. "Go and get dressed since I'm sure that it will take you twice as long."

Oddly enough, she just nods her head and leaves the room. It won't be until I'm lying in bed later tonight, about to fall asleep, that I'll realize that I just told her that I love her.

SAPD SWAT

Aimee

Close to a week later and I'm still freaking the hell out. I mean seriously, who just drops an "I love you" casually for the first time? All I could do was walk back to his bedroom and get dressed in shock.

Worst part is, that for the rest of the day he acted like it never even happened!

I tried to look for any sort of cue that he was waiting for me to say it back and all I got was nothing! He just kept on the entire day like he didn't say something that made my heart simultaneously jump for joy and want to run in fear. He could've given me some sort of acknowledgement so that I would know that I wasn't just going crazy.

But nope, not Declan. He did as promised and took me out for breakfast. While acting like nothing monumental just happened. He was then completely normal the rest of the day that we spent at my place with Stacey and Brad.

I obviously didn't do as good of a job of acting normal, since my two besties kept giving me curious glances the entire time. Well, at least until Declan left. Once he was gone, they pounced on me like a cheetah does a gazelle.

They sat there and gave the appropriate responses of shock when I told them what he said and how he acted afterward. We spent the rest of the evening trying to figure out why he acted as if nothing happened.

The only conclusion that Stacey and I could come up with was that he regretted it and was hoping that if he pretended like he didn't say, so would I. Brad tried to tell us that we were being stupid and that there was probably a much better reason, but damned if we could figure it out.

So, here I sit at the nurse's station, waiting for Heather, yet again, to come in and relieve me after an incredibly long shift. Of course, I'm still freaking out since our schedule haven't synced this week and I haven't been able to see Declan.

I'm now even more convinced that he regrets saying it and is totally avoiding me. I mean it's easy to use work and other things as an excuse. If he does regret it, I wish that he would just talk to me about it. I feel like I'm losing my freaking mind.

A hand waving in front of my face brings me out of my daze. "Hello, earth to space cadet. Anyone home?" Stacey giggles at her lame joke.

I look over and see that she is way too pleased with herself. Ya know, come to think of it, she's been overly cheery lately. Not that she isn't a happy person, but this is a bit much, even for her.

"Why have you been so happy lately?" I grouch like the miserable bitch I seem to be this week.

She raises one of her perfectly manicured eyebrows at me. Seriously, she gets them done every week without fail. "Sorry that I haven't decided to join the dark side like some people."

I lean back in my chair and tap my fingers against the desk. "You're overly cheerful. You're like you but on steroids."

She looks down at her hands and starts cracking her knuckles. Ah ha! That's her tell for when she's hiding something. And like any rational adult, I'm obviously going to jump all over her life so that I can avoid my own.

She looks up and gives me a weird grimace that I'm sure is meant to be a smile. She is the world's worst liar. "Gee, sorry I can't be in a good mood."

I purse my lips. "You're always in a good mood. That's why our friendship works out so well. I'm bitchy and you're sweet. But you're really happy." I widen my eyes and grab onto her shoulders. "The kind of happy and smiley that you get when you've met a new guy!"

I shake her like the crazy person that I am. She tries to move away but I've got a death grip on her and the way to ignore my problems. "Are you holding out on me?"

I get up nose to nose with her and watch as she tilts her eyes to the left before answering. "What? Why would you say that?"

"Why aren't you answering my questions? You're acting mighty shady right now."

She puts her right hand in front of my face and roughly pushes me away. "I'm not answering your question because you're nuts!"

I snort. "That's not an answer. I've been crazy since the day we met. You're totally avoiding my questions since you hate lying and really suck at it."

She gives me a frown. "I do not suck at lying," she huffs. "I can do it perfectly when I want to."

I raise an eyebrow and smirk at her. "If you had to lie to save your life, you'd be dead in under two seconds," I drawl.

"Whatever," she mutters while crossing her arms over her ample chest.

"So, who is he?" I singsong while batting my eyelashes.

"Why are you so convinced that I've met someone."

"Because you only ever act this squirrely when it comes to a guy."

"I don't get squirrely."

"And I'm the sanest person on earth," I deadpan. I lean back and cross my legs. "Look, you don't want to tell me right now, that's fine. Hurtful but fine." I sniff looking for some sympathy and only receive an eye roll. "But eventually you are going to have to come clean."

She purses her lips. "If I was seeing someone," she holds up her hand to stop me from speaking, "and I'm not saying that I am." It's my turn to roll my eyes. "I fully understand that I would have to tell you at some point."

I shrug. "Eh, I'm not too worried about that."

She gives me a dubious look. "Why not?"

I give her an evil grin. "Because if I even throw Brad so much as a smidgen, this much really," I raise my hand and leave a small gap between my index finger and thumb. "A tiny little bone, he'll be all over. We'll know this guy's entire life story in under an hour."

Her face is void of all emotion. "Do you think that if I did happen to be dating someone, that this would be the reason why I wouldn't mention it to you?"

I tilt my head. "No, you should want to know every single piece of dirt that you could."

"You didn't do that with Declan," she grumbles, but she's right, I didn't.

I chuckle. "That's because that man is like a damn open book that just won't close. The only thing that I'm curious about is his word slip last week. Other than that, I know everything about the man who doesn't shut up."

She raises her eyebrow and gives me a victorious smirk. "Even about that woman in town who says that she dated him and that he was awful?"

I take a minute to think. "Does she have a really weird and high-pitched voice?"

Stacey looks uncertain now. "Yeah."

"She's lying."

"How do you know that? Maybe he's lying to you, ever think of that?"

I giggle at her put-out expression. "Nope, I've heard her say that before when I was in line at the grocery store. Her damn voice carries for miles. Anyway, she said that Declan wasn't packing anything large, if you get my drift." She nods her head. "Well, I can tell you that is most certainly not true. Unless that chick is dating Ron Jeremy, Declan would've been the biggest that she's probably ever seen."

Her eyes go wide and she just stares at me with her mouth hanging open. "Seriously?" she mutters and wags her eyebrows.

I laugh at her antics and push her shoulder. "Yes, you weirdo. Now forget that I ever told you that."

Her snort tells me that won't be happening. "Please, anytime I look at him and Damon now, that's all I'm going to be able to picture."

I'm about to respond when I hear the voice that sounds like nails on a chalkboard to me.

"Hello, can you stop chit-chatting about your boring life so that you can give me a report. Some of us have work to do," Heather bitchily says as she takes the seat next to us.

I look at my watch and then give her a saccharine smile. "Wow, look at you, only forty-five minutes late today. Must be difficult to have to cake all that makeup on. Good for you for finally being quick about it."

Heather is turning an interesting shade of red while Stacey has turned her chair around. I can still see her whole body shaking with laughter, so I don't know why she bothered. Well, until I hear the other voice.

"What do you mean 'Only forty-five minutes late.' You just told me that you've been here the entire time, Heather," the voice belonging to Darleen, our Head Nurse, cracks like a whip above us.

"Ah," the dumbass says.

Darleen looks to me. "Is that why you're still here? Is that why you seem to stay late often?"

Now see, if Heather wasn't such an awful cow, I would totally cover for her. Truthfully, I would do it for anyone on the floor...well almost anyone, minus two people.

145

"Yes, ma'am." I nod my head.

Her eyes go squinty. "Does this happen often?"

I chew on my bottom lip and fidget in my seat. Darleen's glare really is impressive. Especially since she's only about 5'3. "Every time she's my replacement."

Darleen puts her hands on her hips. "Why haven't you said anything?"

I shrug sheepishly. "Kimber always clocks her in. I figured that it would be pointless since according to the system, she was here."

If looks could kill, Heather would be a pile of ash right now. I'm not gloating on the inside or anything like that. Well, not too much anyway.

"I see." You could literally hear a pin drop right now. We've garnered the attention of everyone around us. The look of disdain on her face when looking at Heather is something that I will never forget. "Since Kimber is out tonight, I'm guessing that I'll find your actual time clocked in."

Heather just stumbles around with her non-coherent excuses. I'd feel bad if I didn't despise her so much. But truth be told, this is one of the best moments of my life. It's awesome when karma finally does her thing.

"Heather, get to my office now." Darleen's command offers no room for argument.

Doing the first wise thing in most likely her life, Heather gets out of her chair like her ass is on fire. She's gone so fast that she almost seems like a figment of my imagination. Well, until I look up to see Darleen scowling where Heather just made her exit.

Darleen shakes her head and sighs. "Aimee, just hang tight for a few more minutes while I move the scheduling around a bit. I'll try to have you out of here in under thirty minutes."

I give her a smile that I'm sure looks like a constipated grimace. "Sure, take your time" is what I say, while I'm mentally screaming for her to hurry up. Luckily for me, my parents didn't raise an idiot and I just keep fake smiling until she disappears down the hallway.

The minute that she's gone, you can hear the collective snickers from the rest of the nurses and some doctors that are currently on the floor.

Let's just say that I'm not the only one with a dislike for Heather. Granted my hatred goes much deeper than everyone else's. But she's still hated by pretty much everyone on our floor. Kimber is probably the only person who actually likes her.

"Thank God!" Sophie, one of the other nurses exclaims. "Hopefully they'll stick that she-demon on a different floor."

The chorus of "Mhmm's" and "hell yeah's" is freaking ridiculous. If she wasn't such a heinous bitch, it would be really sad.

Thirty-seven minutes later, yes, I counted, and Stacey and I are finally walking out of work. Thankfully, I'm off for the next couple of days.

I plan on enjoying a large glass of wine while gloating and telling Brad everything that happened. I'll make sure to go into extreme detail.

For poor Brad's sake, obviously, since he's out of work. I'm a good friend, just trying to make sure that he stays up to date with all of the gossip on the floor. He would do the same for me.

I hear a snort come from my left and look over at Stacey. She's looking at me with an amused expression and shaking her head.

I raise an eyebrow. "What?"

"You."

I pause half a second at her simple declaration and then continue walking. "What do you mean...me?"

She stops by my passenger side door and waits for me to unlock it. She replies while I fumble around my bottomless pit of a bag looking for my keys.

"I don't even think that you were this chipper after the first time you finally had sex with Declan. And that's saying something because your ass was beyond annoyingly happy."

I look over at her with my mouth agape. "That's rude, especially since you're supposed to be the nice one out of the two of us."

She crosses her arms over her hello kitty scrub top and taps her left foot. "Says who?"

I give her a blank look while still finding everything in my bag except my keys. "Everyone who has ever met us."

Stace gives a weird little hum. She tilts her head to the side. "Why aren't the doors just opening?"

"Because I'm not Harry Potter and this isn't Hogwarts," I deadpan.

"And you wonder why people think I'm the nice one?" she mumbles.

"I never said that I wondered why. I know exactly why and truthfully it works out in my favor. I don't get asked to do half the shit that you do."

"It's nice to be helpful," she huffs while giving me a disapproving look.

"It's also nice to be left the hell alone." My fingers finally snag my keys. "Ah ha! Finally!" I exclaim and proudly hold up my keys.

Stacey gives me a slow clap and then spirit fingers. "Yay."

Like the amazing friend that I am, I ignore her sarcasm and only allow my eyes to go semi-squinty. "And to answer your earlier question," I click the unlock button so that we both can get in. "the battery is dying. The doors won't unlock for some reason unless I actually click the button. I have to get Dec to change the battery for me."

We both get in and get situated before putting on our seatbelts.

Stacey looks over at me as I start the engine. "Why don't you just do it yourself?"

I shrug as I begin to pull out of the parking lot to take us home. "Eh, I like making Declan feel useful."

Stacey starts giggling. "Seriously?"

I shake my head with a smile. "Nope. The last time I tried to open it, I ended up stabbing myself with the butter knife that I was using. I figure that I might as well save myself the trouble since I know that he'll do it for me."

She nods her head in approval. "That makes sense."

"I think so."

"And while you've got him cornered you can talk to him about what he said."

I slouch into my seat. "Dammit Stace. I was doing so well with not thinking about it."

I smell watermelon and look over to see her putting on some Chapstick. "You are going to have to talk to him about it at some point."

I snort. "Yeah, that's a negative. I won't be bringing that up...ever."

She pauses mid-swipe and creepily turns her head to look at me. "Are you kidding me? You're not going to talk to him about it at all? You've been freaking out about it for a week!" She glares.

I pull out of the parking lot and onto the road. "And what if he tells me that it was a mistake? That will be a thousand times worse to actually hear him say that."

Stacey gives me a cluck of her tongue. "And what if he tells you that he meant it?"

I shrug while driving us to our apartment complex. "I guess that I'm just not willing to risk having my heart shattered into dust." I look over at her miserably while stopped at a red light. "My heart wouldn't even crumble Stace, it would be decimated. There would be absolutely nothing left."

Giving me a sad smile, she shakes her head. "That's a bit dramatic Aims. You've gotten over heartbreak before. You can do it again. It will just suck more this time."

I pull into the lot at our apartment complex. "You don't get it. He's my person Stace. I just know it. He's it for me and it's unbearable to think that I'm not it for him. My chest already feels like a sumo wrestler is sitting on it just thinking about not being with him. Ignorance really is bliss sometimes."

"So, you're just going to keep on acting like everything is hunky-dory?" she asks incredulously.

I open my door and start to get out. I look over at her with a small smile. "If it allows me to stay in my happy space with Declan? Yeah, I'm willing to just act like everything is normal."

I get out and close my door. I look over the hood when I hear the passenger door slam shut. "That's an absolutely horrible way to live!"

I start walking, knowing damn well that she'll be right behind me. Thank God we live in different apartments. I'll at least get a small reprieve before she storms her ass back over to my place.

"No, it's called self-preservation. What's horrible is the fact that you actually say 'hunky-dory.' What are you, eighty?"

I unlock the security door and generously hold it open for her. What I would really like to do is close it in her face and catch the elevator up alone. But I'm smart enough to know that would just make it worse.

Stacey is the sweetest person in the world until she's pissed. She doesn't get mad very often, but when she does, it's best to just stay out of her way. It's always the nice ones that are truly the scariest.

We take the elevator up to the third floor in silence. And I can guarantee you that it's not a comfortable silence. Nope, it's one of those that's filled with enough tension that you would need a machete to cut through.

I'm doing the adult thing and looking straight forward and ignoring her very existence. Stacey, on the other hand, is leaning against the wall, arms crossed, foot tapping and a scowl on her gorgeous face.

I will not run out of this elevator like a frightened child. I will stroll off this elevator like someone who is awesome at adulting.

Being a well-functioning adult, I allow her to get off first when the doors open. See? I have totally got life under control.

"I'll be over after I shower and change," she grumbles as she stops to unlock her door.

"Super," I drawl as I walk past her and down the hall towards my own.

I rush into my apartment and shut the door quickly. I lean back against the door and shut my eyes while banging the back of my head a few times. I stand here for a minute, trying to figure out if I can get pass out drunk before she comes back. Can't bitch at someone who is unconscious.

I hear a few manly coughs and chuckles and realize that Brad and I are not alone. I peek through my eyes and yup, definitely not alone.

"Hey hellcat, rough day?" Declan asks with a panty-melting smirk.

I flush bright red. "Eh, sort of. Stacey and I are having a little squabble."

"No Stacey tonight?" Marc asks.

It's then that I decide to look around and see that Marc, Damon, and Danny are here.

I frown at Marc. "Don't you have a home?"

He doesn't even look the least bit offended. "Yeah, but Kay is working late tonight. They have some big build or something."

I look around slyly making sure that nothing is destroyed and hear a bunch of chuckles.

"Don't worry, the four hellions are with Dee," Marc lets me know. Okay, maybe it wasn't so much of a sly look, as it was one of horror.

I toss my bag onto the table and remove my bacteria and God knows what else filled shoes. "I thought that Kayla tries not to let them spend too much time with their grandma. I thought she ends up teaching them bad habits."

The look on Marc's face can only be described as mischievous. "She doesn't. But, since she decided to make fun of my dishwasher organizing skills...again, I decided that the kids could use some time with the world's most awesome grandmother."

I blink at the moron a few times. "You realize that your wife is either going to kill you or you're not getting laid for a very long time....right?" I say slowly.

He shrugs his right shoulder. "I'm pretty hard to kill. Plus, it's shark week, so I'm not getting laid anyway."

I look over at Damon. "Have you gone stupid somehow too?"

"Nah. Doll took Jax and both of our mothers to some baking convention or some shit."

I look over at Danny with a raised eyebrow. "Sage has the girls. I finished with lessons at the gym for the day. So, I decided to see how Brad is doing. I figured that I could help him work out some of the muscles that he hasn't been using."

I give him a genuine smile. "That's nice of you."

He gives me an evil grin. "Plus, Mason called to tell me what tall, dumb and soon to be dead over here did. I figured that I should spend his last hours with him."

"I'll be fine," Marc says dismissively while scrolling through his phone.

We all just look at him and shake our heads. I'll give it to him. That man really is fearless. If I was him, I would not purposely piss off a woman who tried to drown her ex-husband.

Declan leans in and gives me a toe-curling kiss. He leans his forehead against mine. "I'm sorry that you and Stacey are fighting. Hopefully, you two will work it out before you go too long without seeing each other."

Brad and I snort simultaneously, much to everyone else's amusement. Declan tilts his head at me in question but Brad answers.

"Yeah, Stacey will be here in thirty minutes. The only reason that she's not here now is that she wanted to change out of her work scrubs. Those two could fight and draw blood and still wouldn't go without seeing each other." He chuckles while flipping through T.V. channels.

"Seriously?" Declan asks.

I pat him on his stomach because...well abs. "Didn't you ever find it a little odd that we even live in the same apartment building and on the same floor?"

I start walking down the hall towards my bedroom.

"I thought that was just a coincidence," Declan replies.

I giggle. "Yeah, not so much. I told you a while ago that the three of us were a package deal. You should have taken my warning more seriously."

I close my door and make a mad dash to undress, shower and get redressed before Stacey gets here. I love her more than life itself, but I wouldn't put it past her ass to "help" with the Declan situation. I plan to stay in denial for as long as I possibly can.

I'm out of my room and walking down the hallway towards the living room just as the front door opens. Score! Made it.

Stacey and I look at each other with tiny matching glares. You know the ones. Hers saying that I need to talk to him now and mine saying that she better keep her mouth shut. This should be a fun evening, I mentally chuckle.

And it actually is, if you don't take into account that Stacey and I sat on separate sides of the room and still had our mini stare downs. Brad being the ever-dutiful best friend sat in the middle of us like Switzerland.

"You two are seriously going to do this all night?" Marc asks while looking between us.

We both nod our heads because yes, we're both stubborn as hell when we want to be.

Marc looks at the other guys for help and gets absolutely none. "No one else finds this weird?"

"Doll and Mellie are worse," Damon grunts.

"Sage and Kay can put anyone to shame." Danny grins.

Marc looks at Declan for some help. "Don't look at me. You've seen Damon and me when we're both pissed at each other."

"Haven't you've seen Kayla and Sage when they're mad at each other?" Stacey asks him.

He nods his head. "Yeah, but they'll just throw food or something at each other and call it a day. They don't sit there giving each other evil looks all night. What are you both so mad about anyway?"

Stacey says, "She's living in denial" at the same time I go, "She's seeing someone and won't admit to it."

We both go back to glaring at each other except now Brad's interest has been piqued. Thankfully, not about my issues since he knows all about them. Nope, he's heard that our bestie is hiding someone from us.

Have I ever said that I'm a good person? No. Do I try to be better? Also, no. Am I most likely going to hell? Sure, but I'm more of a warm-weather type of girl anyway.

Brad's head creepily turns in Stacey's direction. Judging by the look on her face, she's mentally planning an extremely painful death for me. Huh? I might be getting to that warmer climate sooner than I thought.

"Seeing someone, are you?" Brad asks calmly...too calmly. The type of calm before the storm of him pouncing all over her.

Stacey holds up her finger and waves it around. "Don't even start going all creepy Yoda on me right now. I have my reasons for keeping parts of my life private right now."

I snap my fingers. "So, you admit it! You are hiding someone from us."

"I wonder why she would do that," Declan drawls from beside me.

Stacey gives him a smile, while I turn and glare at him. "Shh, you're supposed to be on my side."

He wraps his arm around my shoulder. "I'm always on your side. But you can't understand just a little why she would want to keep it a secret for a bit? You and Brad are ready to gang up on her like a bunch of toddlers fighting over the last pixie stick."

Everyone just looks at him with wide eyes. "Are you kidding me right now?" I shriek. "Don't think that I haven't heard how you're the nosiest out of the bunch. Lavender told me all about Vegas," I huff.

Declan holds out his arms. "And look what happened."

"They ended up married and had a baby?" Marc asks innocently...too innocently.

Declan looks over at him with a glare. "Don't help me."

Marc gives him a smirk and shakes his head. "Come on now buddy, you know me better than that. You know that I am not trying to help you at all."

"I'm so lucky to have you in my life," Declan deadpans.

Marc nods his head seriously. "I know, you really are."

Brad nudges my arm and tilts his head in Marc and Declan's direction. "And they think that the three of us are weird?" he says lowly in my ear.

I nod my head in agreement. "I know."

Marc and Declan kept going at it for the rest of the evening, amusing the hell out of the rest of us. Well, except for Damon. He kept looking at me like he could see into my head. Thankfully, he stayed true to form and didn't utter a single question. Other people may find it odd how little he talks, but damn if I don't appreciate it some days.

Brad decided to spend the night over at Stacey's, stating that he wanted to give Declan and I some alone time. That may be true but his nosy ass is determined to find out everything he can about who Stacey is dating. And I really do feel bad about sticking him with her. Well, at least until Dec and I get back to my room and he starts undressing.

Seriously, how does his body seem to get better every time that I see it? The man has never met a cookie that he doesn't like and yet his abs are a work of art. It's so unfair that men can eat what they want and look like they were chiseled out of stone. Yet, I even sniff a brownie and I gain ten pounds.

"Baby, what's wrong?" Declan asks.

I shake my head while sitting on my bed watching my own private strip show. "Absolutely nothing. Nothing at all."

He snorts and snaps his fingers at me. "My eyes are up here, *hellcat.*"

I nod my head. "I'm aware of where they're located. But I would much rather look at your abs and ass right now."

"I'm trying to have a serious conversation here."

I blink but for the life of me, I cannot remove my eyes from his lower half. "Can we have that conversation in the morning, when you've unfortunately put clothes on again?"

"Babe, I'm serious."

"Me too," I state plainly.

I mean, come on. What woman in her right mind is going to take talking over staring at her man, when all he's wearing is tight boxer/briefs? No one...that's who.

Much to my utter dismay and annoyance, he quickly gets into bed, pulling the covers up to his chin. I turn and give him a glare. He just raises an eyebrow with an annoying smirk.

I huff and get under the covers as well. No sense in just sitting there since my show is over.

I rest my elbow on my pillow and put my head in my head. "Happy now?" I grumble.

"Yes, very. I no longer feel like a cheap piece of meat."

I roll my eyes. "Don't even try that one. You purposely remove your clothing slowly every time we get ready for bed."

He ignores my comment completely. "What have you been upset about tonight?"

I blink. "You already know. Stacey is hiding who she's dating."

His lips twitch just like his brother. It's kind of cool and creepy to see. "Yeah babe, I let you feed everyone else that line of bullshit. But you forget, I know you, and I know that something else is bothering you."

"Oh really? Now you're observant?" I snark before I can stop myself.

His head rears back and he looks momentarily shocked. "What is that supposed to mean?"

Ah, I really need to think before I speak some days. I shake my head and try to give him a bright smile. "Nothing, it was just a long day at work. I'm just in a bad mood, that's all."

"What haven't I been observant about, babe?" he asks calmly, in a low tone.

I bulge my eyes. "Nothing Dec. You're great, okay? Can we please just go to sleep?"

Does he do as I ask? Of course not! This is Declan that we're talking about after all.

He sits up and frowns down at me. "Seriously Aimee, what's wrong? You've been off all week."

I snort. "Really? Have I? Have I been off all week? I wonder why that is?" The sarcasm is thick enough to hopefully smack him in the head.

"Would I be asking if I knew?" His voice raises in anger or frustration. I'm not sure which but I don't really give a rat's ass right now anyway.

"You should since it's your fault." I cross my arms over my chest and glare up at the annoyingly handsome man beside me.

"How in the hell can it be my fault when I have no idea what I did?" He throws up his arms and quickly lowers them to pull on his hair.

I narrow my eyes. "Think really, really hard Declan."

"I've been trying to figure it out all week. The only thing that I can come up with is that I'm dating a woman who's crazy."

I shove his arm and he doesn't even budge a centimeter, which only adds fuel to my fury. "I am not crazy, you jackass."

He looks down at me. "Oh yeah, no, you're totally sane."

"I would've been just fine this week if it hadn't been for you."

"How can you be pissed at me when I haven't even seen you this week? Are you mad that I had to work and just stayed at my place?"

I chuckle darkly. "That is so not what this is about."

"Then for fuck's sake just spit it out!" he shouts, raising my hackles.

"Fine! You really want to know what you did?" I get up on my knees so that we're face to face.

He gives me an incredulous look. "Would I be asking you if I didn't? I mean shit, I could be sleeping instead of having this awesome conversation."

"You told me that you love me and then acted like you never said it!" I shout like a deranged creature.

We both just stare at each other in silence. The only sounds are of our heavy breathing.

He's just staring at me, blinking repeatedly.

My whole world feels like it's come to a complete standstill. Like even the Earth has stopped rotating because it understands how monumental this moment is. It's out there now and there's no going back. I'm too scared to even breath right now. I can hear my heart pounding in my chest.

"I didn't want to spook you," he states like my whole being is riding on what he's saying.

Now it's my turn to blink profusely. "What do you mean?"

He tugs on his ear and gives me a sheepish look that doesn't bode well for me. "Okay, so I didn't even realize that I had said that until I was lying in bed that night."

My heart sinks to the bottom of a black pit. Any shred of hope that I was carrying flies away with my happily ever after. "So, it was a mistake? You didn't mean it?" I try so hard to sound unaffected but my wobbly voice gives me away.

I go to get out of bed but he wraps his arms around me tightly. "Hold on *hellcat,* that's not what I meant."

I'm unable to look him the eyes right now. The last thing that I want to see from him is pity. So instead, I stare down at my legs. "What did you mean?" I ask, hating how shaky and low my voice sounds to my ears.

He tries to lift my chin but I refuse. "That I figured the next day that it might freak you out if I started saying it to you."

I raise my head to look at him but everything is blurry. Stupid tears. "Why would that freak me out?"

He swipes my cheeks with his thumbs and gives me a wary smile. I nod my head a bit. "Okay, it might've freaked me out for like a day...two tops. But saying it and then acting like you didn't was a million times worse."

He gives me a self-deprecating laugh and rubs the back of his head. "Yeah, so I've never told anyone besides my family that I love them. I guess that I don't really know how to go about this."

"Saying it and then pretending that you didn't is the very, very wrong way," I growl, sounding very much like the angry hellcat that he accuses me of being.

Judging from the glare that is causing my dick to shrivel up in fear, it was a horrible idea to pretend that I never said it. In my defense though, I really had no idea how to proceed after that. In hindsight, I probably should've asked Michelle, Mellie, hell even Kay's salty ass instead of just acting like nothing happened.

I mentally make a note to myself to make sure to text them to see what a good apology gift would be.

I hold my hands up in surrender. "Okay, I understand that...now. At the time, not so much. You have to realize that this is all new to me."

She pouts her plump lips and narrows her eyes at me. "When you say that you've only ever told your family that you love them...."

I nod my head. "Yeah, that's true. Though really, I just say it to my momma and grandma."

She gives me a look of disbelief. "Only them?"

I nod again.

"No one else?"

I tilt my head knowing damn well what she's fishing for but I just can't help myself. "Well, yeah. I tell Damon all the time."

"No other women?" She's turning such a cute shade of red.

"Michelle, whenever I'm in the mood to piss my brother off. I make sure to give her a hug that lasts a few seconds too long for his liking." I smile at the woman who is back to glaring daggers at me.

"Any other women that aren't related to you?" she huffs like a pissed off kitten.

I shrug my shoulder. "Eh, Kay when I feel like pissing Marc off. But her salty ass doesn't play along as well as my wonderful sister-in-law does," I pout.

She throws her hands up in the air. "Ex-girlfriends Declan! Have you said it to any of the other women that you've dated?!" she shouts.

I give her a put-out frown. "Why are you yelling at me? Why didn't you just ask in the first place if that's what you wanted to know?"

The look she's giving me says that I should probably sleep lightly for a while. "I really don't know why I love you. You're a damn nightmare."

I give her a bright smile and wrap my arms around her. "But that's why we work so well, my pissy little *hellcat*. We're both crazy." I squeeze her tight.

She rests her head against my shoulder and gives a long sigh. "You know, when I imagined us declaring our undying love, I pictured it going a lot better than this."

I chuckle. "Yeah, but that's not us. We're the storm, Aims, not the calm before it."

She reaches up and pinches my cheek like someone's annoying Aunt Edna. "Aw, look at you trying to be poetic."

"I have my moments."

She snorts. "Is this going to become a thing?"

I look down at her. "What's going to become a thing?"

"You sprouting off cheesy lines at me."

I pick her up and gently body slam her back down onto the bed. Her giggles are the best sound in the entire universe. I would follow that sound to hell and back, no problem.

I sit on top of her thighs and hold her arms down at her sides. Moving her body, she starts trying to buck me off to no avail. She's so tiny compared to me, that she just looks like a fish flopping around out of the water and I have to swallow the laugh in my throat. But it's cute that she's putting in some effort.

I look down at her with an amused expression. "Aims, what are you doing?"

She growls while still flopping around uselessly. "Trying to get your heavy ass off!"

"How's that working out for you?"

She looks up at me and narrows her pretty eyes. "It would go a lot better if you weren't so fat," she hisses.

Now it's my turn to narrow my eyes at the lying woman under me. "We both know damn well that I don't have any fat on my magnificent body."

If she rolled her eyes any harder, they would get stuck in the back of her head. "Good grief. How do you fit that fat head of yours through doorways?"

I give her a salacious grin. "I'm not sure. But we can see how much of my other fat head you can fit into your mouth."

"Seriously?" She laughs.

I hold up my hand. "Okay, okay. I'll admit, that one was pretty bad."

"If you're going to start trying to talk dirty, maybe you should read some books."

Hmm, I could get down with this. Sure, reading porn isn't the same as watching, but it could have some benefits where Aimee is concerned. "Have any in mind?" I lower my head and run my nose against the side of her neck.

I lift my head and look her in the eyes waiting for her answer. "Not really. Just look for ones with shirtless firefighters on the covers. Those are always good ones." The smile on her gorgeous face is pure evil glee.

I get nose to nose with her. "Take that back right now *hellcat!*" I growl like a deranged beast. "You know damn well that cops are better than those hose jockeys."

"I don't know. They always seem to be in really good shape."

"Well, they should. They don't have anything else to do all day besides workout. And those hose pullers wish they had a body like mine," I grumble.

"Someone's a little touchy." She chuckles.

"You would be too if you were being compared to someone who only has their job because they couldn't pass the police exam."

"Oh my God, you are ridiculous!"

"No, what's ridiculous is the love of my life comparing me to a dalmatian molester."

She lifts her hands to her mouth and gasps out a laugh. "I cannot believe that you just said that."

"What?" I blink innocently.

She pushes my shoulder. "That's horrible Declan."

I nod my head seriously. "You're right."

"Thank you," she says before I've finished.

"I shouldn't insult those poor dogs like that. It's not their fault that they drew the short end of the stick when it came to owners."

"There's something so wrong with you," she mumbles.

I run my hands up and down my chest and stomach. I don't miss the way her eyes track the movement and start to glaze over. "Look at all of this perfection. There isn't one thing wrong with me."

"I wasn't talking about your body." She licks her lips and like it was a light switch to my dick, he is now very much so ON.

"You should be careful about licking your lips like that Aims," I say in a low voice filled with need.

She looks up at me with defiance and licks those luscious lips once again. "And why's that?" The need in her voice matching my own.

"Because I might just give you something else to lick instead."

Her chest is rising and falling rapidly. I can feel her scissoring her legs underneath me. "Why would that be a bad thing?" She bats her eyelashes.

"It definitely won't be for me," I smirk.

She pushes on my shoulders and I take the hint. I roll over onto my back while ridding myself of my underwear at the same time.

She raises up on her elbows and hungrily looks down at my cock. I didn't think it was possible, but I get even harder with the way she's eyeing me like I'm her favorite lollipop.

While she's busy taking in her fill, I decide that I want to do the same. I grab the bottom of her pink camisole and lift it over her head and it's off in one swoop. She shakes her head with a smile. I tug on her black lace panties next. Luckily, she's willing to help me out by removing them quickly.

No matter how many times I see her naked, she still takes my breath away every time. Every inch and curve of her is pure sex.

Her body looks like it belongs in another time, truth be told. She doesn't have the bony structure that women today seem to have. No, she's more of a Bette Paige. She has curves that I love running my hands and tongue over.

She's shaped like an hourglass instead of a pole. I know that she hates her curves but I thank God every day for them. Her ass still brings tears to my eyes when she wears tiny boy shorts and nothing else.

"Now who's licking their lips?" she says full of attitude.

I look up at her and give her a wink. "My tongue is just trying to figure out where he wants to start." I run my hands along the outside of her thighs, up the side of her ribs and straight to her breasts that are more than a handful.

Her head leans back while I massage her breasts. I get a deep moan when I pinch one nipple and then the other just hard enough to bring a hint of pain. I start to sit up so that I can let my tongue explore a bit only to be pushed back down.

She pushes my shoulder down while shaking her head at me. "Nope," she pops her P, "not this time. It's my turn to have some fun."

Being the generous man that I am, I lie back down obediently and put my hands behind my head. "I wouldn't dream of spoiling your fun, *hellcat.*"

She gives a none too delicate snort. "How generous of you."

I nod my head solemnly. "I try baby. I'm all about being a giver."

"You're too kind," she says while leaning down and taking my cock into her small hand.

At the first feel of her tongue on my crown, I lose the ability to form coherent thoughts or sounds. At the feel of her lips sucking me into her mouth, I'm pretty sure that I see stars. When she does this twisty thing with her tongue and hums, I'm pretty sure that I'm going to try to convince her to marry me tomorrow.

"Fuuuuuck," I moan out. Truthfully, it's all that I'm really capable of saying right now.

She takes me as far as she can into her mouth while using her hand to cover the rest of me.

She's twirling her tongue around the tip while simultaneously pumping her hand up and down. She tightens the pressure of her hand on each downward spiral.

Unable to take not touching her, I wrap my hands around her hair. Tight enough to grip onto her but loose enough so that I'm not holding her head in place at all.

She does another little hum and I practically jump out of my skin. Jesus, I can already feel that little tingle at the bottom of my spine.

Fuck that! I refuse to cum before she has though.

I gently tug on her hair, to get her to pop off. She gives me a cute frown when she lifts her head. Well, it would be cute if she didn't look so fuckable with red, swollen lips.

"What's wr..." is all she gets out before I switch our positions. She gives a little squeal as I flip her down onto the mattress.

She huffs when her head hits the pillow. She lifts up onto both elbows and gives me a sardonic grin. "You could've just asked me to lie down."

I shake my head and give her a wicked smirk. "Nah, I like watching the way your boobs bounce. Too bad you don't go without a bra all the time."

She rolls her gray eyes at me. "Yeah, that won't be happening."

I nod my head in total agreement. "I know. Too many stupid motherfuckers with a death wish trying to break their damn necks to get a glimpse of you," I growl.

She shakes her head. "That's not the point I was making."

"It's the only one that matters though."

I decide to kiss her instead of continuing this conversation. No need for me to get irrationally angry when no other man will be looking at her without a bra ever again.

I run my tongue over her lips and she automatically parts them, granting me the access that I was after.

She always tastes sweet, like chocolate, strawberries, watermelon, and something uniquely her. I could drink her in forever and never need anything more. Her kisses could nourish me, mind, body, and soul for eternity and it wouldn't be enough.

I mentally slap myself. Rocco's sappy ass is rubbing off on me. I need to hang out with Marc more. I'm turning into a damn pansy without meaning to.

I release her lips and kiss my way down her body. I lick and suck lightly on her nipples. Her moan of appreciation causes goosebumps to pop up all over my body.

I continue downward and lick around her belly button before continuing on my mission. I kiss and nibble from one side of her pubic bone to the other, eliciting a giggle when I hit certain ticklish spots.

Deciding that she's had enough, she grips onto my hair and non-too-gently pushes my head down. I raise my eyes to hers. "I was getting there."

"Not quickly enough," the smart ass replies.

"Patience is a virtue," I mumble into her mound.

"I'm all out of those," she groans when I swipe my tongue from the bottom of her core to the top.

When her tangy taste hits my tongue, I become like a man starved and dive into her. If her moans are anything to go by, she's happy about it.

As much as I would love to take my time with her, I'm too on edge. I need her to cum so that I can get inside of her.

I circle my tongue around her clit and continuously pick up the pace. She begins to grind herself into my face, causing me to hold her hip down with my left hand.

With my right, I stick one and then two fingers into her. I start off slowly but pick up the speed gradually, trying to stay in sync with my tongue.

I can feel her walls begin to clench and start to pump my fingers in and out of her even faster.

She's making incoherent noises that I'm pretty sure are meant to make sure that I don't stop.

Her walls are tightening so much that I'm barely able to move my fingers, telling me just how close she is.

She moans loudly and her whole body stiffens as she cums.

I slow down my fingers and tongue, trying to draw out her orgasm as long as possible for her. Well, as long as my dick will allow right now anyway.

When her body goes limp, I give her one last long lick and slowly pull my fingers out of her tight channel.

I wipe her juices off of my face with my discarded shirt. I look down at her and smirk at the goofy and glazed look on her face. Nothing makes me want to beat on my chest like a caveman more than when I see what I do to her.

But there's plenty of time to admire my handy work later. My dick feels like he's about to explode and the only place he wants to do that is in her.

I get between her juicy thick thighs that she has left open after going limp. Not that I'm complaining. The less work for me right now, the better. I'm a guy...sue me.

I run my length through her core and make sure that I'm properly coated with her juices. She's more than wet, but I'm still a big guy and the last thing that I would ever want to do is cause her any sort of pain.

But considering that she still hasn't seemed to rejoin the land of the living, I don't think that she would really care either way.

"You ready babe?" I ask just to make sure.

"Mhmm," is all I get with a goofy smile.

I smile at my woman. "You gonna open those pretty grey eyes for me?"

"Maybe later," she mumbles.

Okay then, I mentally shrug. I start to slowly enter her and feel like I'm finally home.

No matter how many times I've been in her, it always feels better and better. Inside of her is my favorite place to be.

She moans and wiggles her hips around once I'm fully seated inside of her. She does this each time to get adjusted to my girth. I just grit my teeth at the sensation of her clenching her walls and wiggling around.

My whole body begins to sweat. Jesus Christ, I'm so far gone already that I could cum just from her getting comfortable at this point.

That won't be happening...ever, but it still feels like it.

Once she lifts her hips for me to continue, I can't even help myself. I pull out to the tip and slam my way back home.

I keep up a brutal pace, chasing the orgasm that I can feel tingling at the bottom of my spine. Her body is bouncing furiously, causing her to put one hand up on the headboard to keep herself in place.

Her bountiful breasts are bouncing up and down causing me to get even harder. Aimee really does have some weird-ass spell over me. Anything and everything about her gets me harder than stone.

I can feel her walls tightening again and realize that she's close as well.

"Put both hands on the headboard Aims. This is going to be fast and hard," I grunt out.

She gives me a smirk and does as I ask. Her eyes are boring into mine as I lift her right leg and cradle it in my elbow.

I start pounding into her with enough force that I can see her arms straining to hold her into place. I use my right hand to rub circles around her clit.

If I'm going to cum, so is she.

My eyes begin to cross when her walls clench so much that it feels like her pussy is vacuuming my dick up inside of her.

Just when I think that I'm not going to be able to hold out any longer, she cums with a high-pitched wail.

Thank fuck! I finally allow my own orgasm to wash over me. It feels like I keep cumming for years instead of a few seconds.

Her whole body goes taut once again before she falls back onto the bed with a sigh.

I let go of her leg and place most of my weight on my elbows. I nuzzle my face into the crook of her neck and just breath her in.

My favorite scent, Aimee and sex, nothing better.

She taps me on my shoulders. "Roll over big guy, you're squashing me."

I kiss her lips and regretfully pull out of my happy place. I roll over onto my side and pull the blankets over us.

She snuggles herself into me, her head under my chin, making sure that my arms are wrapped around her. She places a chaste kiss on my chest, right above my heart.

"Night Dec, love you," she says with a yawn before falling asleep faster than a narcoleptic.

Who knew that four simple words could mean more than any others that you've ever heard before?

I pull her tighter against me and kiss the crown of her head. "Love you too, *hellcat*," I whisper before falling asleep with a smile.

What does not have me smiling is waking up to my phone ringing in the middle of the night...again. Can't I just a peaceful night's sleep with my very naked woman wrapped around me like a damn octopus? Is that really too much to fucking ask for?

I feel a small, feminine hand whack me across the face. "Answer the damn thing," the she demon sleeping next to me growls. I guess I'm not the only one who's pissed off.

I shake my head and reach over to the bedside table for my phone. I fumble for a few seconds but finally grab ahold of the offending object.

I hit the green button. "This better be fucking good," I growl in a voice filled with gravel.

"Just thought you would want to know, some uniforms picked up the guys who jumped Brad in a bar fight an hour ago," my brother states.

That has my eyes opening wide. Sleep completely forgotten. "Say what now?"

I sit up on the edge of the bed and pull on my underwear. I walk into the bathroom and silently shut the door before turning on the light. I wouldn't want to risk Aimee's wrath by waking her up again.

"I just got a call that those homophobic pieces of shit were just picked up in a bar fight."

I run my hand through my short hair. "How did they know it was them? And why were you the one to get a phone call?"

I lean against the sink and stare at my reflection. Looking at myself in the mirror and listening to Dam speak, it's almost like he's right here. Annd, that's fucking creepy.

I decided to close the lid on the toilet and take a seat. My brother and I are weird enough as it is. No need to make it worse.

"Thompson, one of the uniforms on duty tonight has seen the video and recognized them. And I told them to call me so that you wouldn't have to get Aimee's hopes up with each phone call."

I narrow my eyes. "That was oddly nice of you," I say suspiciously. Let's be real here. I love my brother but he isn't overly nice.

"Your point?"

"Why would you care so much about getting Aimee's hopes up or not?"

"You love her," he says simply. "Now, I do too."

His statement would probably sound like some weird wife sharing shit to anyone else but I get it. It's how I feel about Michelle too. He would do anything for Shell, which means that so would I. Twinning comes in handy some days.

I don't bother thanking him because he would just brush it off anyway. So instead, I just get straight to the point. "Why not just call in the morning?"

"Figured that you might want to say hi to them before the station gets overly busy in the morning."

I smile even though he can't see me and ask the only question that comes to mind. "You driving or am I?"

"I'm in the parking lot at Aimee's place already," he says before hanging up.

I get dressed in a rush and sneak out of Aimee's place as quietly as possible. I make sure that the door is securely locked before walking out of the building.

And just as he said, Damon is in his truck waiting for me. It's times like this that make me realize how great of a brother he is. It almost brings a tear to my eye.

I open the passenger door and hop in. I buckle my seat belt and rub my hands together in glee. Dam gives me a blank look before pulling out of the lot and onto the road.

I look over at my best friend. "Anyone joining us?"

"Marc," Damon grunts out.

I smile to myself. Of course, Marc would be there. He just can't help himself most days. I have such good friends, I muse.

We drive the rest of the way in silence. Which is just as well, I need time to get my mind in the game, so to speak. I can't let my emotions interfere with my actions.

I don't want to let my anger towards them cloud my judgment. Honestly, I just want to know why. That's all really. Just why they hate Brad so much that they almost beat him to death.

I just want to know what made them think that they could get away with something like that. Why they had to be such fucking scumbags to a man who has probably never been mean to anyone a day in his life. A man who has already dealt with more pain and anguish in a short amount of time.

So, yeah, it's best that I sit here and mentally calm myself down so that I don't do anything stupid. No matter how much I may want to. That's not what anyone needs, especially Aimee and Brad.

I'm obviously in deeper thought than I realized because the next thing that I know, we're pulling into the lot at the station. I look over and see Marc getting out of his truck with a shit-eating grin on his face.

Okay, I'm not going to lie, I would love to let Marc loose with one of his crazy ass plans right now. Man, would I love nothing more. But unfortunately, we really do need to be smart about this.

Damon gets out of the truck and I do the same. He's shaking his head at Marc. "I already told you that you have to behave."

Marc pouts at my brother, reminding me of one of his kids. "I know, but I'm hoping that Dec changed your mind." He rubs his hands together while looking at me hopefully.

I shake my head and give him a sympathetic smile. "As much fun as I'm sure whatever plan you've concocted is, Damon is right, we have to be good." I can hear the disappointment in my own voice.

I really would love nothing more than to let Marc loose on them. His mind truly is a twisted place some days.

You can see him physically deflate. "Fine," he mutters petulantly before turning on his heel and walking towards the side door of the station.

I just shake my head and smile as I follow him. I swear I feel bad for Kay some days. She's raising five kids instead of four. No wonder her ass is always so salty.

The three of us walk in through the back and get a few wary looks from some of the other officers, while others just smirk evilly.

Okay, so our reputations may be a little bad. It also doesn't help that everyone has heard what happened to Michelle's ex. I still state that was just some weird act of God though. We really didn't have that much to do with it.

Damon walks over and shakes the hand of a uniform officer who looks like he's maybe in his mid-twenties. He's all baby faced with blue eyes and blonde hair.

"Thanks for the call," Damon says to whom I'm guessing is Thompson.

Thompson just shrugs. "Glad that we were able to bring them in. I saw that video." Disgust lacing every word. "I have a brother who's gay. I don't know what I would do if someone did something like that to him. I figured the least I could do was give you a call."

I walk over and extend my hand. "Thanks, man. I really appreciate it."

He shakes my hand in a firm grip and just nods his head in acknowledgment. He tilts his head towards the back hall. "They're all separated down that way. I'm going to go get some coffee. It's been a long night."

Without another word, he turns and walks down the hall towards the break room.

As I stand here and watch him walk away, I realize that I should probably buy him a case of beer as a thank you. And possibly Brad's number for his brother.

"No," Damon growls as he shoves me towards the back rooms.

I nudge him back, which does very little. He really needs to skip the gym every now and then. "No what?"

"No to setting Brad up with his brother."

I scoff. "You don't know that's what I was thinking." I mean it was...but still.

He stops outside of one of the doors and crosses his arms over his massive chest. "Your eyes lit up when he said that his brother was gay."

Marc being used to this particular quirk of ours just leans back against the wall to eavesdrop like the nosy ass that he is.

"That doesn't mean anything," I defend.

"With you it does."

I stand toe to toe with my admittedly, bigger reflection. "How so?"

"You always want people you care about to be happy. You think that setting him up with someone will make him happy again. But he needs to do this on his own, brother."

"At least we would know for sure that he's gay," I mutter, not denying or agreeing with anything Dam said.

My brother grabs the back of my neck and pulls me into him. His eyes bore into mine as he speaks in a low voice. "He had control taken away from him. He needs to regain it when he's ready."

Stupid insightful bastard. "I know. But is it so wrong to want to help him out?"

"It is if he hasn't asked for help."

I back away from my brother and crack my neck. "Fine." I sigh. "But I still think that we should get his brother's number just in case."

"Nah, don't worry about it," Marc casually replies.

Dam and I look at each other and then at Marc. There is no way in hell that he has already gotten it somehow. He's been with us the entire time!

"I'm afraid to ask but I have to know," I reply.

Marc just rolls his eyes at us. "I've seen Thompson and a guy who looks just like him at The Sweet Grind a few times. We can always just have Brad meet us in there one day." He shrugs.

"I feel like that was a bit anti-climactic," I say to no one in particular.

"We haven't gone into any of the rooms yet," Damon grunts out.

I wish that I had known that I had jinxed myself with that last comment. Because nothing could prepare me for what those guys told us. Got to love drunks...right?

I turn my head towards the sound of the door opening and frown when I see that it's only Brad.

"Well hello to you too, sunshine," he greets in an obnoxiously chipper voice.

My right eye twitches. "Why are you in such a good mood?"

He walks to the coffee pot and pours himself a cup. "Oh, I'm not. But you look so grumpy that it made me happy to annoy you."

"I'm glad that I could help," I mumble into the rim of my own coffee cup.

"What's got you so cranky?" He takes a seat next to me on the couch. Both of us in sweat pants and over-sized t-shirts. Aren't we an awesome pair? "Declan not hitting the right spots?"

My eyes narrow and I shove him with as much effort as I'm willing to use. Which in all honesty, isn't a lot since the caffeine hasn't kicked in yet. "No, it's because he snuck out of here at four-forty-five this morning and woke me up."

The cup pauses mid-way to Brad's mouth. He slowly turns his head in my direction. "What the hell was he doing at that time of the morning?"

I shrug and tuck my legs underneath me. "I don't know. He got a phone call that he took in the bathroom. He got dressed and snuck out like a teenager trying to get to a rager."

Brad scoffs. "He's not cheating on you."

I snort and nod my head. "Yeah, no, that thought didn't even cross my mind." And it's true. That is just not something that he would ever do.

Brad blinks a few times before raising an eyebrow that's even better manicured than mine. "Then why so glum, chum?"

"Seriously?" I drawl.

He waves a hand around. "Fuck off. I haven't had enough coffee to be witty yet."

"I don't think that you've ever had enough coffee then."

His eyes get squinty. "Watch it, bitch. I'm pretty much all healed. I'm definitely healed enough to cut up some leggings and those ugly ass Uggs."

"Do it...I dare you."

He rolls his eyes and stretches his legs out onto the coffee table. "Don't dare me to do things that I would do gladly." He takes a sip of his coffee. "But if you don't think that he's cheating, then why are you all grumpy?"

"Because I'm pretty sure that he's probably out doing something stupid with his brother, or Marc, or both. How bad is it going to look when I have to bail him out of the same precinct that he works at?" I huff.

"Eh, I wouldn't worry about it too much," he replies calmly.

"And why is that?"

He rolls his head in my direction and gives me a smirk. "Because, according to everyone else, they're pretty adept at staying away from jail time."

"That makes me feel so much better," I deadpan.

"It really should. Sure, he'll probably do something dumb, but at the end of the day, he'll still be here. Hopefully with some pizza."

"All you do is think with your stomach," I grouch.

He blinks at me innocently. "What? I'm a growing boy."

"The only thing growing is your fat head," I mutter.

I get up and walk into the kitchen. I place my empty mug into the sink. I turn to look at Brad. "I'm going to go get dressed in case he does need to be bailed out. Or in case he gets back early enough to take me out to breakfast as an apology for sneaking out. Either or."

"And I'm the one who thinks with my stomach?"

I stop at the mouth of the hallway and put my hand on my hip. "At least I'm not sitting here hoping that someone else's boyfriend will bring them food."

He sniffs. "I don't think that I'm ever going to date again. Single is going to be my new norm. Guys don't even interest me right now."

I quirk my lips. "Is that why you've been watching *Aquaman* so much lately? Because you have no interest in men right now?"

"I like the acting. They did a really great job," he lies horribly.

"Right. I'm sure that it's going to win an *Oscar*."

"Jason Momoa's abs should." I raise an eyebrow. "It doesn't count when I drool over him! Everyone in the world does." He has a point. I've seen that movie several times and it's not for the acting.

"Whatever. I'll be in my room if you need anything...like a new box of tissues."

"Shut up," he grumbles but doesn't deny it, making me chuckle the entire way to my room.

I strip out of my baggy clothes and throw on a cute pair of jeans, a white shirt that says: *pumpkin is the spice of life,* and my black and white chucks. I look in the mirror at the jeans that are making my ass look incredible and smile.

I decide to do my hair in two pigtail French braids. Let's just say that Declan complimented that look...a lot. Luckily, I've gotten pretty good at it and it only takes me a few minutes, as opposed to the hour it took me when I first started doing this style.

As I'm swiping on some mascara, I hear a knock at the front door. Hmm, Declan must've forgotten his key. I'm about to put on some lipstick when I hear a woman shouting. That's weird. It's probably one of our neighbors being pissy about something, I mentally shrug.

I'm about to ignore it when I heard Brad shouting back. Jesus, we're going to get written up for a noise complaint if they don't keep it down.

I put down my makeup and almost walk past my phone on the nightstand as I make my way towards all the commotion. Luckily, the display lights up with Declan's name as I pass. I grab it and hit the green button on the way out of my room.

"Hey babe, can I call you back? Now's not really a good time," I say into the phone as I walk down the hall. The yelling is getting louder the closer I get.

"What's going on over there?" Declan's tone is worried.

I'm about to respond when I hit the end of the hallway and see a woman pointing a knife at Brad. And not just any woman...his mother.

"Brad's mom is here with a knife," I speak without thinking. If I had thought, I wouldn't have said anything since she didn't see me. Unlike now, while she's staring between Brad and me, whirling the big ass *Michael Myers* looking knife around.

"Hang up!" she screeches. Her voice sounding completely unhinged.

I do as she says since I'm pretty sure that Declan has caught the jest of it anyway. Hopefully, there will be a lot of nice police officers here soon. Preferably before she stabs us.

"Ah, hi Mrs. Whitman." Honestly, my mind is kind of drawing a blank right now but apparently, my mouth just won't quit.

Brad looks over at me with wide eyes and mouths '*hi?*' like I'm stupid but I kind of am right now. It's not every day that your best friend's mother shows up wielding a damn knife. Cut me some slack.

She freaking hisses at me. "You shut up too! You're no better than he is." She points the knife at Brad while venom laces every word. Okay then. "Both of you go sit on the couch!"

We raise our hands and slowly walk to the couch. I can see my phone light up with Declan's name. Yeah, I'm not going to be able to answer you right now babe. I put it in my back pocket right before I sit down.

Brad grabs my right hand and squeezes it. I can feel him shaking as we hold hands. I'm not much better either, so I can't really say anything.

His mother looks completely unhinged right now. She's normally extremely well put together since Mr. Whitman expects nothing less. But today her hair is a rat's nest and her very modest dress is wrinkled beyond belief. It looks like she slept in her car or something.

"Mom, what's going? Why are you doing this?" Brads voice quakes towards the end.

The look of loathing she gives him is beyond shocking. It actually causes my breath to hitch. There is so much menace in her eyes that it's one of the most frightening things that I've ever witnessed.

Gone is the meek, mild, and beaten down woman that I've met in the past. This woman is full of venom and rage. She also looks like she's out for blood. Blood belonging to my best friend and me now unfortunately as well. What the actual fuck?

Well, she's still beaten down judging by her cut lip, black eye, and swollen cheek.

"What's going on?" her voice deceptively low and calm, causing goosebumps to break out all over my body. "What's going on is that my son is a fag and your father has been blaming me for it for years."

"I don't understand," he says sadly.

Her dark chuckle is like nails on a chalkboard. "Of course, you wouldn't. You're the one living like a heathen and I'm the one getting punished for it. All because I gave birth to YOU," she spits out.

"Why would dad punish you?" he asks and truthfully, I'm kind of curious as well.

I mean let's face it. Mr. Whitman is an asshole on the best of days. He's the type of sack of shit that likes to hit people just to make him feel better about his own pathetic existence. I'm just curious as to what his reasoning is.

Her grip on the handle of the knife tightens. Her knuckles turning white from the force. "Because I carried you, gave birth to you and according to your father, babied you so much that I turned you gay!"

I snort without meaning to and receive a menacing glare from *mommy dearest* over here. "You can't turn someone gay. It's just who he is."

"It doesn't matter to his father. His only son is gay and that's all that counts. I'm the one who gave birth to Brad and cared for him, so it's my fault."

Brad tries to stand but Mrs. Whitman jabs the knife towards him. He stays seated with his hands up in the air. "Mom, you know that it isn't your fault. It isn't anyone's fault. It's just who I am. It's a natural part of me like my hair and eye color."

"Natural?" Her laugh is even more unbalanced than before. "There is nothing *NATURAL* about you. It is not natural to like other men. God states that marriage is for a man and a woman ONLY!"

I wonder if she's really paid attention while reading the Bible because there are definitely some sketchy things that go on that would prove her wrong here.

She starts pacing back and forth like a caged animal. "And once you and your sister left, he had no one else to take his anger out on about you being gay and your sister whoring around at that *school*. I'm the one who has to take the full force of his anger."

"Mom, just stop. You know that Elle isn't whoring around. She's in college for business management. And you could've left years ago, just like we did." Brad chuckles but it holds no mirth. "If would've been great if you had left and taken us with you when we were kids. You know, before he started kicking the shit out of us."

She stops dead in her tracks and stares at him with her mouth agape. "And where exactly would we have gone, Bradford? My parents made me marry your father, so I couldn't go to them. I haven't been allowed to work a day in my life and barely finished high school. So, please tell, how was that going to work?"

He shakes his head sadly. "I don't know mom, but you could've tried something."

Her eyes light up eerily at that. "I did!" She smiles maniacally at him.

He scoots a little closer to me. "What did you do mom?"

I wonder if she killed Brad's dad and is now here to kill us. It would work with the whole level of crazy that she's got going right now.

She resumes her pacing and starts talking, almost more so to herself than to us. "Well, I sort of did anyway. It's not my fault that those guys didn't finish the job."

My hands automatically raise to my mouth and tears start forming in my eyes. I look at Brad and see that he's trembling beside me. She cannot be saying what I think that she is.

"Finish what job mom?" he asks in the most dejected tone that I've ever heard.

She swivels around and looks at him with a huge smile. "To kill you, of course." She rolls her eyes like it's the dumbest question that she's ever heard. "If you're dead, then your father won't have anything to be angry with me about anymore. I already do as he asks, you were the only thing that I've ever done wrong."

I honestly don't know what to feel right now. I'm so angry that his own mother did that to him. Angry at all of the pain and suffering that she's caused him.

But at the same time, I feel so incredibly sad for her. This woman has been stuck living under someone's thumb her entire life. Dealing with years upon years of physical and mental abuse.

I hate her but I also understand her. Everyone has a breaking point. It was only a matter of time until this broken doll shattered.

"Why go after Brad? Why not kill his dad?" I hear myself asking before I can think better of it.

If that was me, I would get rid of my abuser, not one of my children. But hey, that's just sane old me.

They both blink at me like I'm a weird science experiment. But eventually, Mrs. Whitman shakes her head. "I need my husband. I don't need a gay son who has caused all of my problems," she says so simply that my heart breaks for Brad.

I couldn't imagine my parents ever doing anything to harm me. My parents would even apologize for yelling at me when I was bad. They would literally give up their own lives for me.

"Is that why you're here then mom? To kill me because those guys didn't?"

"They should've killed you!" she screams. "I even told them to hit you in the back of the head to make it quick." She looks at him with a sweet smile. "I didn't want you to suffer honey. It was supposed to be a few hits to your head and that was it. But they didn't listen. They were even bragging about how they made sure to keep you alive throughout the whole beating."

What the fuck do you even say to that? Luckily, she continues on her creepy ass rant so we don't have to say anything.

"But did they listen to my directions? No. How difficult is it to follow directions? I always follow directions. It makes life so much easier always knowing what you have to do. Bad things like this are what happen when you don't follow directions."

She continues on with her creepy mantra and pacing. While she's distracted, I nudge Brad with my elbow. He looks down at me and raises an eyebrow.

"We have to figure out a way to get that knife away from her," I mutter out of the corner of my mouth. "There's no telling what she's going to do."

He gives me a sad look but nods his head. "How would you like to do that without getting stabbed?" he mumbles.

I shrug. "I don't know. Can't you just tackle her or something?" He is the guy in this scenario.

His eyes narrow. "Yeah, sure. Let me just tackle her while she's holding the knife. I'm sure I won't impale myself on it."

"Well, distract her or something before you make your move."

"How would you like for me to distract her? You know, since you're coming up with such stupendous ideas and all," he drawls lowly.

I widen my eyes. "I don't know. Tell her how much of a mess she looks. You've said how much your dad hates that and how she always has to look good."

He looks at her and then back at me. "She's a little past that point, don't you think?" he hisses in my ear.

"Well, I don't see you coming up with any bright ideas," I huff.

"Neither are you."

I choose to ignore his sarcasm since we're both in a very stressful situation. "Just throw something at her then."

"I don't see that working out since both of us have the athletic ability of a toddler."

"It'll be fine. Just throw something really wide, that way you won't miss."

"And what will you be doing, since I'm doing all the work?"

I blink at him. "I'll be sitting here rooting you on. Ya know, moral support and whatnot."

"You can't at least throw something to distract?"

I shrug my right shoulder. "You were the one who just said that I don't have any athletic ability. Plus, it's your mom. If mine was in here being a psycho, then I would deal with it."

Just as he's about to answer with what I'm sure is some sort of smart-ass reply, we hear sirens outside.

And even better, the sirens distract her so much that she runs to the window with her back to us. Brad and I look at each other and I tilt my head in his mom's direction.

I pick up one of the gaudy silver candlestick holders that my mother *insisted* that we had to have in our apartment and hand it to Brad. Thank you, momma, for your horrible taste.

He's looking at me like I'm crazy. "Just hit her hand that's holding the knife, not kill her, you big baby."

He gets up and slowly creeps up behind her with the candlestick holder in his hand. She whirls around just as he gets behind her. Her eyes widen to see him so close and she goes to stab him.

Thankfully, working out with Danny has seemed to improve Brad's reflexes because he dodges her hand and whacks it with the holder.

She screams out in pain and drops the knife. I jump up and rush over to them. I make sure to kick the knife out of the living room.

She's on her knees holding her wrist and crying. "Why couldn't you just die? Now he's going to be even angrier with me that I won't be home to make his dinner." She sniffles.

Wow, just wow. I would love to slap some sense into her but I have a feeling that's how it all got knocked out.

But Brad being the absolute sweetheart that he is, just gets down on the ground with her and wraps his arms around her. He keeps caressing her hair while trying to get her to calm down. "Shh, it'll be okay mom. We're going to get you some help. I promise." I hear him whisper as I walk into the kitchen.

I take out my phone and see a ridiculous amount of missed calls from Dec. Just as I'm about to hit send another call from him comes through. "Hey babe, we're okay."

"Thank fuck!" His tone is nothing but relieved. "What happened?"

"Brad's mom had a knife. Long story, but we got it away from her. You guys might want to come up though."

"I'm already on your floor," is all he says before the line goes dead. Would a goodbye kill him?

The door opens and all I see is Declan rushing in towards me. He's in his full SWAT gear and all I can think is *"Damn he looks good."* There is just something about a man in all black with guns attached to him, wearing a Kevlar vest. Yum.

The minute he sees me, he sprints towards me and picks me up in a crushing bear hug. I wrap my arms and legs around him. Well, as much as I can with all of the stuff that he's wearing.

"Are you okay Hellcat? Did she hurt you?" he asks while trying to look me over.

I place my hands on his cheeks and force him to look at me. "I'm fine babe. She didn't hurt us. She just ranted the whole time about how Mr. Whitman beats her because he thinks it's her fault that Brad's gay."

He gives me a kiss that would make my knees wobble if he wasn't holding me. He places his forehead against mine. "I was so fucking scared that something was going to happen to you. You can't scare me like that Aims. I love you too much to ever lose you. You're never leaving my side ever again."

I pat the big sweet dope on the cheek. "As sweet and as totally un-stalkerish as that sounds, you were the one who left my side this morning." I put my hand over his mouth when he tries to reply. "And as much as I would love to stay in your arms, my best friend just found out that his mom tried to have him killed. Brad needs me a little more than you do right now babe."

I kiss his lips chastely and tap his shoulder to let me down. He does so, begrudgingly.

"Yeah, I've got some stuff to take care of too. Go on and be with Brad baby."

I give a little, definitely not awkward at all, wave to the other guys and walk over to where Brad is standing. He has his arms crossed against his chest as he's watching his mother get handcuffed.

I walk up and put my arms around his waist. He places his around my shoulders and we stay like that for a while.

The next few hours are just a whirlwind of questions and a major information dump.

Down at the station we learned, well Brad, Stacey and I, since the guys all knew, that Brad's mom had hired guys from her church to attack and kill Brad.

Apparently, she found the most homophobic ones that she could. She then told them that the best way to lure him out was with the ruse of a date. His poor sister thinking that she was being nice to his mom, has been keeping her updated on Brad's life. Including that he had joined an online dating app. Elle is going to feel so horrible when she finds that out.

The icing on the shitastick cake was when Brad's father stormed into the police station and demanded that his mother be released immediately. According to him, his wife was *"doing God's work by trying to get rid of the fag"* and that she should be thanked instead of arrested.

Needless to say, that went over about as well as one would expect it to. On the plus side though, Brad did finally stand up to his dad. His dad who promptly ended up in a cell for taking a swing at not only Brad but a few other officers as well. What? I'm a bright side kind of girl.

Now, we're all at Declan's house. Well, I suppose mine now, since he has decided that I was moving in. No asking or anything. Just told me to pack my stuff and that everyone will be over this weekend to help me move.

I was going to try to at least put up a fight until Stacey got all happy and decided that she would take my room so that Brad doesn't have to live alone. It was actually weird how fast she said it.

But whatever, I mentally shrug.

So, everyone is here sitting around, eating pizza, and drinking. While only keeping half-assed eyes on the kids running around. Which is bad considering the kind of trouble that Kayla's kids are able to get into. But Dec doesn't seem overly concerned, so I'm not going to worry myself.

"I still can't believe that they ended up in cells next to each other." Stacey chuckles darkly. She may feel bad for Brad but she is beside herself with joy over the fact that they have gotten what they deserve.

I'm not going to lie, I'm pretty damn happy myself.

"It's not that surprising. My dad needs someone to make his meals without my mom around. It's kind of fitting really," Brad states simply while twirling his bottle of beer around in his hand.

I rest my head on his shoulder. "You okay?"

190

He puts his head on top of mine. "Yeah, I'm okay. Just still in shock, I guess. My dad, sure, he's a horrible asshole. But I guess I just never expected something like this from my mom."

"Everyone has a breaking point. Unfortunately, your mother reached hers," I tell him.

"And that just makes me feel guilty," he says glumly.

"Why the hell do you feel guilty?" Damon barks out. But it's a good question. Brad's never done anything wrong.

Brad leans back against the couch and just stares into space for a minute before answering. "I feel bad that I didn't take her with me when I left or when Elle left for college. We should've taken her away from him. Maybe everything would've been different."

My poor sweet friend. He was the one who was almost beaten to death and yet he's the one who feels guilty. I swear, some people really don't deserve to be parents.

Stacey rubs his arm. "Honey, you know that she would never have left him."

"I know. I swear that I know that. I just can't help but think that I should've done something to help her."

JJ leans forward in his chair. "This may not seem like a good thing. But at least with her in jail, she'll be away from him. She might even be able to get some counseling to help her through everything."

"I guess you're right."

Kayla answers her ringing phone and blinks a few times. "Can you repeat that again please?"

We all look over at the constipated look on her face.

"Okay, I'll be right there. No, don't bother calling him. I'm with him right now. Okay, thanks. Bye."

Kay just sits there for a minute with her lips pursed.

"Babe, everything okay?" Marc asks.

She nods slowly. "Yeah, we just have to get to the hospital."

"What happened?" Sage asks.

"Kellie called," Kayla starts before being interrupted by Rocco.

"Wait, my sister Kellie? Why is she calling you?" Rocco asks.

"She called from Mason's phone."

"Why is she with Mason?" Rocco growls.

"Will you just shut up and let me talk?" Kay asks in a snippy tone that causes Rocco's mouth to snap shut. "As I was saying," she side-eyes Rocco before continuing. "Kellie called me from Mason's phone. I didn't understand much since she was crying. But I guess there was an accident involving Mason and a nail gun. They're at the hospital now."

"Why is she crying over Mason nailing himself with a nail gun?" Marc asks with a smile that is just too wide. Poor Mason is never going to live this down with Marc as his brother-in-law-ish.

Kay does a half cough, half laugh into her hand. "Ah, yeah, see, I think that she shot him with the nail gun on accident. She just kept saying that she didn't mean to press the button."

Everyone just stays silent for a moment to process that information. "Is he okay?" Rocco asks cautiously.

Kayla nods her head with a quirk of her lips. "He's not dying if that's what you're wondering."

The evil gleam in Marc's eyes makes me feel really bad for Mason. "So, where did she end up shooting him?"

"I don't want to tell you guys."

Danny leans forward, almost falling out of his chair to look at Kayla. "Why's that KayKay? Why wouldn't you want to tell the people who think of him like family?"

We all look at Danny with skeptical smirks. "Too much?" he asks and we all nod.

Kay bows her head in defeat and mumbles, "Because she shot him in the ass."

My man practically pushes me aside. "I'm sorry, oh salty one, can you please speak up a bit? Where did she shoot him?"

"In the ass, you nosy ass!"

Marc and Danny jump out of their seats like their asses are on fire. Declan and Rocco following closely behind.

"Where are you guys going?" I ask.

Marc looks at me with what I assume should be an innocent look that's anything but. "To make sure that Mason is okay. He's family."

"I should make sure that my sister is okay," Rocco says with mirth filled eyes.

I look at Danny who smiles unabashedly. "I haven't drunk anything, so I should be the one to drive."

I look over at my man who just scoffs at me. "Come on *hellcat,* you know that there is no way that I'm missing this." He walks over and bends down so that we're eye to eye and gives me a toe-curling kiss. "Love you, I'll be home later!"

He's by the door before I even open my eyes, much to everyone else's amusement.

"Declan, be nice!" I chide. "Poor Mason is probably in pain and doesn't need your annoying ass making it worse."

The dope that I love grabs his chest. "It hurts my feelings that you think that I would be anything but helpful."

I just shake my head and say a prayer that they've given poor Mason a ton of drugs. He's going to need it to deal with all of them. No one should be forced to deal with Declan, Marc, and Danny when they're in pain. That's just wrong on so many levels.

Epilogue

Two Weeks Later:

We've finally just finished moving Aimee into my place and we decided to stop at Home Plate for a beer and some wings. For real, how she had so much shit is beyond belief. Where she kept it all, is a damn mystery.

Our freakishly large group sans the kids, sit down and wait for Morris and Damon to get back with the pitchers of drinks.

I smile and hum a little tune to myself earning an odd look from Aimee. She nudges me with her sharp little elbow. "What are you so happy about?" she asks me.

I look down and smile. "I can't be happy that the woman I love is all moved in?"

She raises an eyebrow. "Not this happy," she drawls.

"You'll see," I mumble to her. I ignore the wary look she gives.

See, I had an ulterior motive for coming here tonight. I happen to know that my favorite bartender is working. And what better time to make everyone eat crow then when we're all together. I wouldn't want anyone to miss out. I'm really nice like that.

Dam and Morris sit down and pass out the drinks. I pour myself a beer and take a healthy sip. Damn, that's good. Definitely what I needed after moving all of Aimee's shit today.

Kayla gives me a curious look. "You are in too good of a mood."

"You say the sweetest things MSG," I drawl.

Unphased, she continues. "No, you're like downright gleeful. You only look this way when you're about to get into trouble or something."

Everyone stops what they're doing and look at me with varying degrees of wariness. Well, except for Marc who looks excited about the prospect of doing something stupid.

"Relax, I'm not going to do anything."

All I receive is blank looks. I just shrug and go back to my beer. They'll see.

And right on cue, Erin walks over to say hi.

"Hey guys, it's been a while since you've all been in." She smiles brightly at everyone.

"We spent the day moving Aimee into Declan's place," Marc says and then looks between Aimee, Erin and myself. It's like taking candy from a baby with these fools.

Erin just looks over at me and Aimee and smiles. "That's great! Congratulations!"

"Thank you." Aimee smiles back.

"Thanks, Erin, I appreciate it," I reply.

Erin points her thumb in the direction of the bar. "Well, I better get back to work. Do any of you need anything while I'm here?"

Everyone looks at each other with different looks when really the only way they should look is guilty. These lying asses having this bet going on forever.

"Yeah, actually, it's probably time to settle up the bet," Marc states. "You won since he just announced the move on your week." He hands her an envelope with what I assume is filled with cash.

Erin reaches out, takes the envelope and starts counting the money.

Damon looks over at me. "You ain't even curious as to why he handed her money?"

I shrug. "Not really." Because I already know, you traitor.

Erin counts out half and passes it over to me. I gladly take it with a huge smile. "Nice doing business with you." She winks at me before turning on her heel and walking away.

"You knew?" Rocco asks in shock.

I give them all a bland look. "Yup. We decided to keep it going for as long as possible to make sure that we get as much money out of you as possible."

"You've known the entire time?" Kayla asks. "Why didn't you say anything? I felt so bad about this bet!" I raise an eyebrow at the little liar. "Not overly bad but still bad," she huffs.

"I can't believe that you pulled it off all these years," Marc says looking astonished.

"I can't believe that ya'll still haven't caught onto the fact that Damon isn't the bad twin."

The looks on their faces were priceless and will stay with me forever.

Eight Years Later:

"Hurry up guys." I plead with my six-year-old sons. Yeah...twins. I'm pretty sure that my mother jinxed me when she would say that she hoped that I would have kids like me someday. "You need to finish that ice cream before mommy gets home."

They really do. Aimee will kill me if she finds out that I let them have ice cream before dinner. But I just couldn't say no to those big grey eyes of theirs.

They look identical to me, except for their eyes. Those eyes are all their momma. Something that pisses my wife off beyond belief. According to her, since she carried and gave birth to them, they should look like her. Too bad for her my awesome genes are dominant. Actually, it's too bad for both of us, because they are me on some fucking crack.

They are way worse than I ever was. I know everyone says that but it's true. Damon and I were angels compared to these two demons. Thankfully, Aimee was smart enough to make me get neutered, as she puts it, after they were born. I shudder to think what life would be like with two more of them.

Brayden and Kayden, don't judge me their names were all Aimee's doing, look at me while slowly licking ice cream off of their spoons. "Why?" Kayden asks.

I lean forward in the kitchen chair, still making sure to keep an ear out for my wife's car, and place my arms on the table. "Because this treat won't be our little secret if mommy comes home and sees you eating it."

Yeah, yeah, yeah, I know, I'm going to hell. Trust me, this doesn't even register compared to some of the other shit that I've done in my life.

"Mommy says that we're not supposed to have secrets from her," Brayden tells me.

Brayden and Aimee are like two peas in a pod, where Kayden is all me. Nine times out of ten, when the boys get into something that they weren't supposed to, Kayden came up with the idea. Brayden being a good brother just follows along.

I drum my fingers on the table. "It's okay when it's a daddy and his boys' secret."

They both blink at me and shake their heads. "Mom said those are definitely not okay," Bray says before shoving a huge spoonful of chocolate ice cream in his mouth.

Now it's my turn to blink. "What?"

Kayden nods his head. "Yep, mom said that we can't have secrets with you because it means that you did something bad that mommy won't be happy about."

I can't believe Aimee would say that to them. Okay, granted, she has pretty good reasons, but still. She has absolutely no faith in me. Again, she really shouldn't since I just can't seem to help myself some days.

Prime example, me sitting here trying to get them to finish up the huge bowls of ice cream that I gave them thirty minutes before dinner. But damn, she could at least pretend to trust my parenting skills.

Just as I'm about to say something, I hear the sound that I'm dreading to hear...Aimee's car pulling into our driveway. I look at the boys' chocolate-covered faces and realize that there is no way in hell that I'm getting out of this one.

Maybe I should take off my shirt and try to distract her with my abs, I muse. She's still as obsessed with those as she was when we met almost a decade ago. I look at the boys and realize that's probably not going to work.

I hear our half boxer, half pit bull, Rocket, going nuts barking and jumping at the front door. That boy is definitely a momma's boy. When Aims is home, Rock is never more than two feet away from her. He loves us all but

Aims is his world. She swears that it has nothing to do with the fact that she spoils his ass with treats.

The door opens and I can hear Aimee giving Rock some loving. I then hear the footsteps that signal my impending demise. The moment Aimee walks into the kitchen the boys' chocolate-covered faces light up like the night sky on the fourth of July.

"Mommy, daddy gave us ice cream," Traitor one, I mean Brayden exclaims.

She gives me a glare before smiling at our boys. "I can see that."

"He also told us to keep it a secret from you," Traitor two tells her. Seriously, where is the damn loyalty in this family?

I purposely keep my eyes straight ahead. I have no need to look at what I'm sure is a menacing glare that she's giving me. "Did he now?"

"But don't worry, we're almost done," Brayden tells her.

"And just in time for dinner," she deadpans. The sarcasm going over their heads but unfortunately not mine.

I look up and give her a big smile. "Have I ever told you how beautiful you are?"

"Every time you've done something stupid."

"Doesn't make it any less true."

"Declan?"

I look up and bat my eyes ridiculously at her. Her lip twitches but I get nothing else. "Yes, my gorgeous, sweet, forgiving, loving...did I mention forgiving wife?"

She rolls her eyes at my pathetic attempt to get on her good side. "Get the boys cleaned up while I get dinner ready."

I hop up and get the boys out of their chairs. "Your wish is my command."

"Mmmmm," is all she utters before turning away. With any luck, she'll forget about it.

Judging by the glare that I'm still getting a few hours later after putting the boys to bed, I'd say not. It also didn't help that they barely ate two bites each of their food.

I sit down on the couch and pull Aimee's feet into my lap. When in doubt, a foot massage is usually a good way to go. Especially for a nurse who is on her feet a ton.

When the boys were born, she considered staying at home but she just couldn't give up nursing. Though, she only works part-time now, so she can still be with the boys a lot. I think it was a great idea personally. If she was at home with them twenty-four-seven, she would've lost her mind.

I start massaging her sock covered feet and ignore what her moan does to certain body parts. Even after all this time, all she has to do is look at me and I'm ready to go.

Even after having the boys, she is still the sexiest woman that I have ever seen. Her curves got even curvier, which she hates, but I love. Especially her ass and her boobs when she was breastfeeding. I mourned a little bit when she decided to switch the boys to formula.

She looks at me from where she's lying across the couch. "What were you thinking Dec? Sweets before dinner?"

I give her a sheepish smile. "I was thinking that I can't say no to their grey eyes any more than I can say no to yours?"

"Don't even try to be cute right now."

"Like I have to try," I scoff.

"Declan," she growls giving my twin a run for his money.

"Yes, *Hellcat?*"

She shakes her head. "What am I going to do with you?"

I wiggle my eyebrows. "I can think of a few things."

"That's so not happening tonight." She snorts much to my disappointment.

"Can't blame a guy for trying," I mumble while resuming my massage.

"The only thing that's happening tonight is me eating my weight in popcorn and becoming one with this couch."

I raise an eyebrow. "Rough day?"

She leans her head back against the pillow and sighs. "Yeah, a young thirteen-year-old girl came into the E.D. with stomach pains. Turns out that she was pregnant and didn't know. It ending up being an ectopic pregnancy and she was taken into surgery. I found out later on that the girl's uncle had been raping her for years. Some days I just can't take how horrible people are. That poor girl."

I stop rubbing her feet and open up my arms. "Come here Aims."

Without hesitation, she crawls into my lap and rests her head on my chest. "I'm sorry that you had to deal with that."

My beautiful, sweet and caring wife looks up at me with tears in her eyes. "I don't even care about me. It's that poor girl. She's going to have to live with this the rest of her life. All because her own family is a disgusting piece of shit." Aims sniffles angrily.

I run my hands through her hair like I know calms her. "I hear you, baby. But, hopefully now, she'll be able to get the help that she needs."

"I hope so."

I keep rubbing her head until she falls asleep. I look down when I hear her cute little snore and smile.

I never would've believed that this would be my life. A wife that I love beyond what I ever thought was possible. Two sons who fill my heart and soul with so much joy that it's ridiculous. A dog that's cool when he's not up my wife's ass. And an extended family that has grown exponentially over the years.

Ten years ago, I never would've thought that this would be my life. I sure as hell didn't think that I would land the hot nurse who I had asked to frisk me. But here I am and I love every minute. I can't wait to see what the next ten brings!

The End

Please consider leaving a review. Any and all feedback is appreciated. Even if you just leave a star rating. Every bit helps other readers find the book.

I love getting stalked by readers! Sign up for my Newsletter to stay up to date! Follow me on Facebook, Instagram, Twitter, Goodreads, and Bookbub!

Newsletter

Bookbub

Facebook

Instagram

Twitter

Goodreads

Website

About the Author

Nikki Mays is a pen name that was created from her maiden name. She is a wife and mother, who lives in a small town in New Jersey.

She has been with her husband for a decade and is surprised that he's still alive.

She began writing as a creative outlet after becoming a stay at home mom. She decided that she needed something exclusively for herself, not just being mommy.

She has two crazy boxers that love to keep that *"Evil"* mailman out of the yard. Besides writing and spending time with her little hellions, she enjoys cooking & baking.

Nikki loves to be stalked by her readers and encourages all interaction.

Made in the USA
Monee, IL
21 April 2020